THE
BLUE DEER
AND OTHER
DREAMTALES

THE
BLUE DEER

AND OTHER
DREAMTALES

DAVID RAINS DAHL

CAPRA PRESS
SANTA BARBARA

Book and cover designs by Frank Goad, Santa Barbara.
Cover background from a painting by Peggy Wirta Dahl.

LIBRARY OF CONGRESS CATALOGUING-IN-PUBLICATION DATA

Dahl, David Rains, 1946-
The blue deer and other dreamtales / David Rains Dahl.
p.   cm.
ISBN 0-88496-433-7 (alk. paper)
1. Fantastic fiction, American. 2. Dreams—Fiction.   I. Title.
PS3554.A2668B58   1998
813'.54—dc21   98-8785
CIP

Capra Press
P.O. Box 2068
Santa Barbara, CA 93120

Dedicated to the memory of my mother & father
Patricia Ruth Rains Dahl
Wilhelm Stanley Dahl
to
Jorge Luis Borges
& Octavio Paz
and, as always, to
Peggy
who shares the path
and the dream.

CONTENTS

Contents

FOREWORD

*T*HE GENESIS OF THESE STORIES begins in dream journals kept over two decades. Thus, as with the nature of the brevity and enigmatic quality of dreams, there's minimal plot and character development possible in such a quick tale; nor is there an internal attempt at analysis or interpretation by the characters or author, who stays close to what the dream says and does. Each brief narrative operates more like a fable or zen *koan* than the more familiar short story. These "sudden fictions" have been inspired by the prose poems of Max Jacob, the "palm-of-the-hand" stories of Kawabata, tales of Nasrudin, that Sufi "fool," the work of Italo Calvino and Julio Cortázar, and those parables of Kafka—to list just a few progenitors.

Dreams *are* stories, but by and for whom? And to what purpose? Who is the "teller?" Who are these strange or familiar characters populating bizarre or ordinary scenes? Where and when does the action take place? It should be clear that attempts to answer these questions with a psychoanalytical "overlay," be it Jungian or Freudian, has nothing whatever to do with the stories-as-stories themselves. They exist as received, in awe and wonder, and it is in that spirit they are passed along. If there is a collective unconscious, as I imagine there is, it's up to the individual reader to ascertain. For myself, I regard these dreamtales as *gifts*, as adventures not only received, as a radio is a receiver, but also actively experienced, and as praxis—remembered, used, related. They may be "healing" but not therapy. The distinction lies between art and science, objective and subjective points of view. Of course, these boundaries are blurring these days, where physicists and mystics convene, but a dualistic way of describing the world is the heritage of our language. (No need to get into all *that*.)

It should be emphasized that the "I" is not the author's I. This may be obvious, but for some it is not always so. The preponderance of first person singular functions to enhance and facilitate, hopefully, an *immediacy*, a direct entrance into such a brief tale. If the story "works," the I becomes a reader's I, who completes each story with a psychical experience, be it of marginal interest or something more, dare I say, *spiritually* profound, a catharsis. Of course, this is how all art comes into being and operates. I regard *The Blue Deer* as a primitive form of *dream sharing*, not so much to communicate a "message," but to say: "Here I am. This is what's happening with me. (Or us!) What can we learn here?"

That said, dreams aren't the sole material in the crucible. The stories aren't all verbatim transcriptions of dreams, yet the majority are close. The bones are dream, the rest is fleshed out with waking experiences, especially from Viet-nam, which feels like a dream to me now, as well as other contemporary, domestic events. The use of Jungian-style active imagination, as well as "shamanic journeying" as taught by Michael Harner, are two essential methods of operation, expanding on the lead of the dream itself and following its contours.

The axiom that the truer something is the falser it sounds is an interesting paradox when dealing with dreams and fiction. I direct the reader to the work of Jorge Luis Borges, whose modus operandi was exactly in that twilight zone where the real, the fictional, the mythic, and the dream overlap and nourish each other. He's the *maestro*, and I've dedicated this work to him; as well as to Octavio Paz, because of his recent passing and my debt to the limpid freedom of his surrealist vision—its elemental eroticism and trail-blazing prescience.

Another facet of dreams as "reflecting the stories of our lives" is my conviction they are also "about" our *deaths*—through dreamwork, paying attention to dreams, we familiarize ourselves with the "beyond," if you will, allowing the transition through stages from life to death, from the known to the unknown, to be more easeful, less a traumatic shock. This process is found in many ancient teachings, including *bardo* journeys of *The Tibetan Book of the Dead*, the Egyptian thanatologies, as well as native oral traditions around the world. I am sympathetic such practical instructions in conscious dying are indeed valid and useful, and that it isn't necessary to wait until one's death bed to begin "dying practice," which is what dreamwork can imply. Elisabeth Kübler-Ross, Stanislav Grof, and E. J. Gold have pioneered a way for us in these matters. Another theme alongside the "death journey" throughout *The Blue Deer* is the scenes of borderlands, crossroads, or labyrinths, where anything is possible, where magic and mystery abound, where the living and the dead make contact, where transformations of body and spirit occur.

I also refer the reader to the work of James Hillman, especially *The Dream and the Underworld*, for a most appropriate and relevant approach to dreams. Many fine books are available on creative dreaming and active imagination as means of understanding self and world *(anima mundi)*. A few authors found helpful: Henry Corbin, Robert Bosnak, Patricia Garfield, Carlos Castaneda, Gaston Bachelard, Marie-Louise von Franz, and Carl Jung, especially his autobiography and *Mysterium Coniunctionis*. Joseph Campbell's *The Hero With A Thousand Faces* has accompanied me on many travels. For the shamanic aspect, I recommend Harner's *The Way of the Shaman*, and *Shamanic Voices: A Survey of Visionary Narratives* compiled by Joan Halifax. Both have excellent bibliographies. The field is wide open, with numerous ways available. It may seem exotic, but shamanism is the root of religious experience, as Mircea Eliade masterfully demonstrates in his groundbreaking *Shamanism: Archaic Methods of Ecstasy*. Dreams and storytelling are not simply potential "methods" but are catalysts in the revelation of the meaning of our lives.

"He comprehended that the effort to mold the incoherent and vertiginous matter dreams are made of was the most arduous task a man could undertake, though he might penetrate all the enigmas of the upper and lower orders: much more arduous than weaving a rope of sand or coining the faceless wind."

—JORGE LUIS BORGES ("The Circular Ruins")

. . .

we must dream backwards, toward the source, we must row back
      up the centuries,
beyond infancy, beyond the beginning, beyond the waters
      of baptism,
we must break down the walls between man and man, reunite
      what has been sundered,
life and death are not opposite worlds, we are one stem with
      twin flowers,
we must find the lost word, dream inwardly and also
      outwardly,
decipher the night's tattooing and look face to face at the noonday
      and tear off its mask,
      . . .

—OCTAVIO PAZ ("The broken waterjar")

INTO THE LABYRINTH

*T*HERE ARE NO HEADSTONES yet I know this is a graveyard enclosed by a stone wall atop a hill containing a grove of gnarled yews. In the twilight something glitters in the grass—retrieving an old sword, I begin brandishing it about like Cyrano as I duel my many foes, who spring at me from behind every tree and shadow. Bored, I attempt to stick the blade in the ground but it simply bends. It's a cheap tin sword, although it had felt hefty and real just a moment before. Then a short bald man in an odd tunic approaches, takes the sword and sets it on the ground in a precise manner, saying, "The sword must always point towards the grave."

I apologize for taking the sword from his grave and pointing it in the wrong direction. He replies, "It's not *my* grave the sword must point to." He then sits, folds arms and legs, and looks straight ahead, as if waiting. I sit near, wondering what's up. A ripple in the tall grass catches my eye, perhaps a snake. Instead, an iridescent lizard emerges wriggling towards me, wide mouth showing rows of sharp teeth. I fear it will bite, but I do not move. When the lizard's within arm's length I swat it away, finding it more annoying than dangerous. The bald guy chuckles, says, "Well done."

I take out my wallet and remove a photo of myself posing heroically in an Army uniform holding a machine gun astride a sandbag bunker. As my companion takes it in his little pink hand, I notice now every time I look at him he changes—sometimes an elderly, round balding fellow, or childlike and cherubic, or "robust," a man at full strength of his powers. He stares at the photo, shoves it back, says, "Clueless then, clueless now."

Annoyed with his cryptic one-liners, I hand him another photo of a gathering of soldiers sitting around a fire at a memorial service in a jungle clearing. Everyone in the picture is old, wizened, white-haired. Merely glancing at it, he chortles, "Auld lang syne, *la la la la la.*" Angry, I leap up, intending to flee from him and this place. However, instead of standing, I rise out of my body and float upwards! At first, I think I'm simply lightheaded from rising too fast, but then as I float higher, I see *myself* far below, and in conversation with what appears to be a large white dog.

At that instant, I've moved on to another place.

THE WORD

I'M PLAYING CHESS WITH AN elderly Jewish man, a chess master, but he can't remember what the chess pieces transform into, so I think he can't be much of a master. He peers over through filmy eyes and inquires in a slow cadence, "Who does the trappist change into?" Confused, I reply, "The Trappist? Like a monk of a Christian order? Or do you mean a fur trapper? Maybe you're imagining a trapeze artist?" "Don't know," he shrugs. I begin to suspect this is either a clue or a slip-up, possibly he's setting a trap for me, so I make my next move as wisely and cautiously as the hourglass permits, at the same time keeping my trap shut.

He then withdraws a book from a satchel at his feet. He says it's called *The Wailing*, also known as *El Grito*, and announces, "Now you'll learn how to read!" I frown, on my guard, peering at the fat book he's opened before me, yet amazed I "get" that it contains magic words, like "AZZA" and "YADDO" along with illustrations of "YAL" and "YOD." These words are both totally foreign as well as an integral part of me, buried deep in my body's memory. I observe a picture of a tree, each leaf a circle of letters, each branch a stream of light. There's the sense of not reading this book, but that *it* is speaking directly into my brain—its magic resides in the fact it is a living thing. And I wonder if reading is something you don't *do*, but something that is done or happens *to* you.

Glancing up from this marvelous book into the wrinkled, monkey face of my opponent, I ask point blank, "How might the knot of ignorance be cut with serpent power?" (Alluding to my tenuous knowledge.) "Don't know, don't know," he sing-songs. And thus with a theatrical gesture, capturing his queen with a pawn, I exclaim, "Yow!" understanding the trap he'd set. He howls with glee, and rolls on the floor, casting signs and symbols into the air, visual notes of music, sublime odors of sound and number, abstracted images and spirits of ceaseless Creation, the One and the Many.

CINÉMA VÉRITÉ

OUR STORY SURVIVES WITHIN the lengthy shadow of Tradition. It can't be helped, we're caught in the grasp of a giant, parrot-beaked squid! Meanwhile, the Captain has not been seen for days and the crew is nervous. I can't keep them in line, they're smashed most of the time, and have become nasty, putting cigarettes out on the expensive props, ruining scenes with drunken carelessness, arriving for work out of costume. They're constantly fighting amongst themselves, and I fear a few have been murdered and thrown overboard.

The harpoonist startles me as I'm applying a bike-tire patch to a tentacle. Moustache dripping foam, he snarls, "You better cut the crap, Mister, or I'll slit your throat!" Drawing a finger across his throat for emphasis. I reply in my firmest Officer's voice, "Now listen, if you'll be patient awhile longer the Captain will return shortly with more beer and pizza." This mollifies him for the moment, yet he returns to his rowdy mates shouting, "The squid's a fake! It's *all* a fake!"

The consequences of this revelation are more serious than you might suppose. The mere *mention* of fakery can destroy a hard-working author's career, confine us here in this leaking submarine *ad nauseum*. Thus, I have no choice but to kill off the entire crew. And recommence in a large, colorfully-striped balloon, soaring through the blue sky, sailing high above the clouds—on our way once again!

The Captain drops another bag of ballast, turns and grins with a twinkle of fiendish cleverness in his eye. He's quite mad you know.

SYZYGY

*A*IMLESSLY WANDERING STREETS of a European city I spy a gilt door at the end of a short cul-de-sac, with *CURIOS* carved on it. Upon entering, I am overwhelmed by a shop crammed floor to ceiling with an amazing array of "curios." The room is so dense with an accumulation of objects it is difficult even to move around and browse. I must turn sideways to get down aisles, such as they are. Picking up a rubber gargoyle, I give it a squeeze, causing it to squeak in a funny way that makes me laugh.

The proprietor, a rumpled gent, white hair fringing a pink dome, glances over bifocals around a precarious pile of books on his desk, and croaks, I presume to me, "You should be aligned with the syzygy tonight." Startled, I nevertheless respond, "When?" "At two," he says, "when the moon is just visible through the clouds." I ponder his words as I examine the aggregation of artifacts, antique toys, medieval scientific instruments, various unfamiliar gadgets, time pieces of all kinds, prototype cameras, ancient maps and globes, astronomical devices, boxes of gems and odd stones, lenses of many shapes and sizes, dusty curiosa, tins and jars containing fascinating objects I do not have words to describe.

Returning to the old man, I peer over the heap almost burying him and inquire, "If I should align with the syzygy, may I purchase that book, the one you snatched from me?" (He'd seized it from my grip with a bony hand as soon as I'd uncovered it from a tangle of cobwebs beside his desk. But not before I'd seen its gold-stamped title, *Mia Innamorata*, and decided the red morocco binding was certainly centuries old. I'd also had a chance to view the frontispiece illustration of a maiden sitting near a pool admiring her reflection, only it wasn't *her* face staring up from the water.) But the old wizard simply stares in bewilderment, as if meeting me for the first time, like our earlier exchange had not occurred.

Determined to return again to barter for the book, I leave that stifling shop, stepping out into bracing night air. Back at the hotel, I enter a steam-filled room, my beloved soaking in the tub. There's the scent of rose oil mingled with sulphur. Squinting through this fragrant mist towards the open bathroom, I can barely see, yet do just make out a white hand, waving to me through the steam, like a sea gull appearing through a fog. And I smile, imagining what will happen next.

THE EAGLE

*T*wo MEN LEAD ME THROUGH a wilderness of thick chaparral, oak and pine. One man is short and stocky, the second slim, with thick braided hair; both have matted beards and are outfitted in animal skins fringed with beads and tassels. Each wears a feathered hat and moccasins, including myself. We don't carry weapons or packs. There seems to be another man, a fourth, but I don't see him, only sensing his presence behind or sometimes beside me.

The intent of our expedition, they've intimated, is to initiate me into an "eagle society," but I don't know what that means, nor do I recall how I've come to be on this trek with these sullen fellows. But I do feel this is an important "rite of passage." Nevertheless, as I stumble along trying to keep up, I wonder if perhaps this so-called eagle society isn't a hoax, and I've been conned into believing it exists? Maybe I'm hypnotized or drugged? Anyway, my bewilderment is real—in a daze about "ordinary" reality. I'm definitely out of sync, and it's all I can do to tag along at the fast pace they've set through rugged terrain without any noticeable trail.

For the whole hot, exhausting day we work our way up a dusty slope without trees for shade, zig-zagging around impenetrable clumps of manzanita. Eventually, just at sunset, as I'm about dead, we must scale a huge boulder, many stories high, sitting by itself on a desert plateau we've reached at the summit of the slope. During the grueling rigors of this last push, I continue to dwell on my doubts about the sincerity of my companions—their authenticity as guides for my "initiation," still thinking this adventure is a put-on, a show for their odd amusement.

And they've certainly provided no clues—the entire hike has been in total silence. My dazed sensation persists.

After what was for me, but obviously not for them, a most painful climb, one which I have absolutely no idea how I managed, we finally attain the level top of this monstrous rock. Collapsing on its hard surface, gasping for breath, I stare into the sky, notice the rising moon is *blue*; then realize with a start, it isn't the moon, but the Earth itself! I can clearly make out the continents of North and South America. Instantly, my doubts begin to waver as I feel revived and energized, although remaining uncomfortable. The strangeness of this experience is overwhelming, like being very drunk and woozy all of a sudden, but not having had anything to drink!

One man builds a fire, motions us to sit near and to remove our shirts and shoes. Then the two stand and stretch their whole bodies, from fingers to toes, as if we'd been sitting for a long time, but to my perception was but a few moments. Without a word or glance at me whatsoever, they walk directly over to an edge of the rock, a sheer side opposite the one we'd climbed. Stunned, I watch the shorter one leap out into space as if doing a swan dive into a swimming pool! I scramble over on all fours, hoping he hasn't killed himself. Seeing him in a contorted position far below, I yell down, asking if he's broken anything. Despite the distance, I can distinctly see his distorted face peering up—the intense, ferocious stare of a wild animal. I become frozen to the spot, trembling uncontrollably.

With a jarring voice, the second man orders me to follow, as he too leaps off. I shout, "No! Wait! I'm afraid of heights! I can't jump. I'm not ready!" Then, a jolt of electricity shoots through me as I notice a fourth man at my side, the one I had only sensed, like a shadowy witness to our journey.

I scrabble away before he can push me off, quickly stand, run a few steps and jump straight upwards, flying in an astounding vertical leap, not only over his head but also out over the two men below. Gliding through the air I hit the ground in a sprint, hundreds of feet beyond the men, now both on their feet doing a grotesque jig of a dance, like huge birds flapping awkward wings. Halting my run, I turn to see the fourth man, still perched atop the giant rock, silhouetted within a corona of light, the radiant blue Earth full behind him. I watch transfixed as he extends his arms and lifts off, soaring as an eagle does, spiraling ever higher and higher, soon disappearing into the darkness beyond, like a vague memory, or a dream that fades with the dawn.

RISE AND SHINE

$\mathcal{M}$Y BED'S ON THE EDGE OF A cliff above the sea. A transistor radio blares near my pillow. I half-listen to a news report about "a preemptive strike" assuming it means an attack with nuclear warheads. My father grabs and shakes my foot, tells me to rise and shine, and go collect another animal to keep the caged leopard company. "Yeah, yeah," I groan, not ready to get up just yet. Rising onto an elbow I squint out across a green lawn that stretches to the horizon. Mesmerized, I watch a black dot far away become a man in a tuxedo walking crisply towards me to set a platter of steaming oysters, mussels, and clams on the bed, turn and march away. Breakfast? I wonder, now fully awake and slipping into the day's disguise.

Shambling over to a pile of newspapers I begin the morning routine—separating out comic sections, the only "bed" the leopard will tolerate. Moving to the cage, I climb in and sit down beside the sleeping cat. My high-school girlfriend is there ratting her brown hair before a cracked mirror. She peers over her shoulder, bats long curled lashes, and coos, "My breasts smell wonderful this morning. You interested?" I respond, "Sure," and crawl over to her corner of the cage to sniff her, admittedly, fragrant breasts. Today they have the sweet scent of over-ripe cantaloupe. I slur "Thanks" and return to the leopard's side to awaken it with a loud shout.

Later, after drinking tequila "in a sacred manner" with my pals all afternoon, I realize I have chores to do, so I buy a pop-up book of animals for dad and a mirror for my girl. Dad frowns as I hand him the book, but, that's to be expected. In the cage, my sweetheart's rearranging her clothes after a typical mauling by the leopard, now snoring blissfully on a pile of shredded Sunday funnies. In a low seductive voice, she says, "Anoint my hair with fire, please." Using a forefinger, I draw radiant white streaks through her "do," leaving a bright, star-burst patch in front. She smiles contentedly, sighing as she turns to preen herself in her new mirror.

Back to bed on the cliff, I examine weird seaweed-like polyps that have sprouted all over my body, then eat the shellfish, still steaming hot, and intended for supper, not *breakfast*! I must speak to that man tomorrow morning, if there is one.

REMEMBRANCE

*E*XCITED BEYOND BELIEF, a man unearths a crystal skull imbedded in a wall of a prehistoric city. As soon as he cleans the skull he finds himself instantly flying like a great bird, soaring above a twisting road of this ancient citadel, past crumbling walls and buildings, then out across a plain, up over mountains to an even more desolate area in a hidden valley. Below him are many dome-shaped mud huts arranged in concentric circles around an eroded monolith. Then everything goes black, he senses a skip in time like a missing heartbeat, and a crack of light breaks open, through which he sails out over an ocean of seething white water. And all becomes dark again.

The man awakens inside an infinitely larger version of one of the round huts, as if the dome of the sky were made of mud. Sitting up he's aware of a Presence, a sure sense a deity inhabits this place. A deep voice startles him: "What do you require?" Fully alert, the man rises awkwardly, shocked to find wings hanging from his shoulder blades! Holding out his hands, his amazement increases—he has paws like a bear with long curved claws. He's become a wingèd beast, a mythic animal he's seen carved in stone. The voice repeats in a firmer tone, "What do you angels *want*?"

Swaying, unsure of what to say, the man answers, "I'm no angel. I'm a man." The voice chuckles, "You may persist in your folly if you wish. Anyhow, you have an obligation to transmit my words to others of your race, since they are apparently incapable of directly hearing me. As *you* are at this moment. Now, say what it is you desire." The man clears his throat—the words leap from his heart, "We require less suffering. Less pain."

The thundering voice laughs again, says, "Your *patience* is your soul. Most importantly, remember your death, and remember Me! Now begone. The Time of Fire is far from over." The man falls to his knees on the floor of the great hut, his broad wings collapsing around him, and sobs.

Opening his eyes, the man kneels before the wall he's excavated, holding a dirt-caked human skull in his quaking hands. Setting the skull down, he reaches around with both hands, feeling for something on his back. He doesn't wonder why. Placing the skull in his pack he trudges to his jeep, sensing a powerful Presence everywhere, in everything, above as below.

THE LIONS

*T*HERE ARE THREE LIONS IN the house, one huge male with a flaming black mane, and two sister females. On Sundays we shove them from the living room, which they've appropriated for their den, into the bathroom for their ritual baths. Getting each into the tub is a difficult messy process, but absolutely necessary, as their musky smell is overpowering and we must wash them down periodically or be driven out of our house. Although they snarl and fuss, the lions enjoy being lathered up and scrubbed with a long-handled bath brush, especially the male, who purrs with husky delight when being toweled down. Afterward, he's all fuzzy and "electric."

Also on Sundays, after washing the big cats, we go for a drive in the family cars. My wife and I in the sedan, the lions in the station wagon. The male lion sits in the driver's seat with a serious, intent expression on his long face, his big paws delicately placed on the steering wheel as he cautiously maneuvers his way through city traffic and out onto the country road. One female rides up front, the other in back, each intently scanning the passing scenery, curious about everything, keeping sharp eyes out for game.

The lions often drive to the same place, a secluded grassy spot beneath old oaks, where we picnic and take African Dreaming Pills together. These are intended to keep our heads clear as we enter a temple that appears in view, also a result of the pills. We sit on a blanket within the temple's central chamber and take turns reading the glyphic tales painted on the walls. The lions know much more than we do, and are only too proud and pleased to interpret The Meanings for us. They often laugh in their strange growling way at our ignorance, but we take no offense, knowing they aren't being mean, and only wish us well.

TWILIGHT OF THE GODS

*S*OME PAST FRIENDS HAVE gathered at a banquet reunion. Soon inebriated, I'm playing a concertina while kicking up my stockinged feet atop a grand piano. The pianist, Duke Ellington, would like me to get off, but is a good sport and plays along. Beneath the piano are two "alligator" women snorting "kaleidoscopes." So I naturally join them. We complain about this "profane trip." But, as it was scored from a nonbelieving priest, what can you expect? The sushi chef points his samurai sword at us under the piano and laughs, then drags us out and says gruffly, "Take seats or no eat."

I'm sitting next to a sad-eyed Vogue-model type wearing a dress made of clear plastic wrapped around living butterflies. On the other side of me is a small shrub that bursts into flames when I address it. I excitedly tell the model about this, but she just sniffs and looks away, as if I smell badly. I say to her, "This is where the little monsters come in, you know." She still doesn't respond, too busy gnawing a leg of lamb still on the lamb. I tell her, "You realize, you don't have to know what you're doing to practice *karma yoga*." She turns towards me, winks, and a little pink monkey leaps out from between her breasts! I catch the squirming critter mid-air and say, "Desire, yes, always."

After the reunion ends with an orgiastic food fight, I'm out in the parking lot caressing a sweet old lady. The Hell's Angels roar up on their choppers. One of them shouts, "Hey! That's *my* old lady!" And threatens to clobber me. I stomp up to him, spit on top of his shiny bald head and slap it. We roll around on the asphalt until I'm sufficiently dirty and grimy. Then the gang accepts me and we have a fine time randomly breaking stuff and pummeling strangers.

Walking home in a rainy mist, I flip up the collar of my red nylon James Dean jacket, enter a convenience store to buy condoms. I tell the clerk in my suavest voice, "I'll require your largest size, miss." She screeches, "Comin' right up, sweetie!" as she rummages through a drawer, then carefully places loose pieces of a wooden puzzle on the counter like they're extremely fragile. It takes some time to assemble the pieces into a box that opens into a tableau—with Death on the inside, represented by skulls, a cemetery, ghosts, etc., and Life on the outside, symbolized by flowers, birds, blue sunny sky, etc.

Stepping outside, I'm confused—not having purchased the condoms as planned, instead I buy a puzzle-tableau, for which I seem to have paid a large quantity of cash. Striding briskly through the rain I dodge into a corner bar. A bunch of nouveau-Nazis are standing around a table staring at a map of Disneyland. I squeeze in, saying, "How's the ol' Weltschmerz coming along?" They look at me incredulously. Finally, one breaks the awkward silence, saying, "I shot ein Gorilla." Not quite hearing what I thought I heard, I extend my hand. Crouched on my palm is the Vogue model. She instantly leaps up and down, waving her arms and screaming in a mouse-like voice, "Run for your lives before he bores you to death!" I laugh sheepishly, put her, kicking and thrashing, back in my breast pocket, then exit the bar with a loud, "Adios! See you at Ragnarök!"

Next day at lunch I'm telling Charlie Parker about a great idea I have for a bebop symphony that would express the *essence of the blues*. But he's pretending to be bored. That Bird!

THE TURN

*D*RIVING ALONG THE COAST at night in a Volkswagon bug, my wife dozing in the seat beside me, suddenly, for no apparent reason, I crank a fast looping U-turn! I notice deep well-defined ruts across the center-divider grass, as if many other cars had done a similar thing in this exact location. And, I can't see straight. It's as if my fast counter-clockwise turn has shut down half my vision, and spun my brain; and I'm trying to correct this by forcing my vision back towards the right, clockwise. But the effort to "straighten out" my mind, as well as the car, only results in more dizziness and intensified fear. It seems *half* of me has fainted.

Soon we're not on the highway anymore, not on any road at all! And my vision's so skewed I beg my wife to take the wheel. But she's no longer by my side, somehow she's popped into the back. Only the right side of my sight is visible. The left side of the world is a complete blank, gone. In the flash of the headlights I see men and women reach towards the car as it bounces and skids through a field of dry grass, a prairie— so unlike the rocky coastline we'd just been driving along.

I finally manage to slow the bucking car—pressing brake pedal to the floor we come to a sliding, dust-churning halt. Taking a deep breath, I warily open the door and step out. A crowd of people dressed all in white immediately surround and grab us. They have on old-fashioned loose shirts, white pants and white cowboy hats. The U-turn seems to have spun us not only into another country but into another time period as well. I'm not sure whether these folks want to hurt or help us. But I am convinced, if I could just turn my vision back clockwise, we'll be all right.

One of these ghostly men grabs my arms and kisses me on both cheeks, saying in an affectionate tone, "Welcome home, brother." His breath smells of burnt rubber and gasoline. Then I watch helplessly as a bunch of them carry my wife off on their shoulders, like a rag doll floating on a cloud of these white-clothed people. Before fading into that dark horizon where empty plains meets starry sky, I see her stare back at me with a look of wide-eyed amazement, rotating her hand in the air with forefinger extended, in an exaggerated, clockwise motion.

SISTERS

*N*OWADAYS I LIVE IN A MEDIEVAL city of stone streets, high walls with port-hole windows, heavy wooden doors. It has become necessary for me to decide between two women, one of whom is an ex-wife. The other lady is of royal blood, an ancient family line, or so she says. But I'm not convinced, as she will not reveal her true name. Not knowing who she is causes chronic anxiety. Both women are attractive, enticing, with raven-black hair and exotic eyes. I often get them confused. There's also the matter of a mistaken adultery. Thus my desire to choose, once and for all, so as not to feel so disconnected. Truth is, I already know I don't want to see the ex-wife again. It would be pointless. She's too moody, a brooder, a dweller in the barrenness of her Fate. The other I look forward to visiting as often as possible. So, perhaps there's no problem after all. Where does this scattered feeling come from, if that's the case?

I take a carriage to the house of one of them, but find her parents standing in the arched doorway with stern, unyielding looks. Their gargoyle demeanors indicate they surely won't allow me to come near their daughter. As I stroll on, I see her jump from a side window, then signal from beneath a bush. Pretending to be just passing by, I casually wave to her guardians, duck around the side, to join her with a big smooch. We make-out right beneath their grim stares. Glancing around, I notice a number of jungle cats sprawled about the yard. They seem to be dead, or perhaps asleep, I can't tell, and wonder why they're strewn across the lawn, draped over branches, and fences? And here I am with this woman again, but I'm still not sure which of the two she is. And she refuses to answer my questions, remaining enigmatic. We decide to slip away and go to an inn, *The Sphinx*.

She's wearing an ankle-length gold-lamé cape, and her hair's in an unusual style, like a woven castle atop her head. I have on a collarless white shirt that hangs below my waist, my legs and feet wrapped with gauze. We take a table, but before we order, I snatch a quill pen and slip it into my shirt, hoping to take notes about this escapade that might help me identify her. A stranger with a baboon-like face comes over. He has a lioness on a leash and announces to us, "Because this animal is now so tame, it's almost human!" I wink my one good eye at him to indicate my comprehension. Then I see other large cats, cougars, panthers, leopards, sleeping on the floor, under tables, on the bar. Or perhaps they're dead? I don't know. But trying to divine more, I ask my mysterious companion if she's ever been to Luxor, to a temple near the Hall of Judgment. She laughs sweetly, then whispers, "There are hundreds of temples in Luxor, my love." Perhaps she's the other? As I pursue this thought, she grabs the feather pen out of my shirt, tickles my nose, then mimes weighing my heart with it.

I think back to my season in North Africa, when I had climbed the outer staircase of an ancient tower discovered in an oasis. A bright crescent moon illuminated the scene. The top opened out onto a bazaar of small shops. A slick salesman accosted me, woofing in my face, to sell me a painting on papyrus of a semi-nude woman in the desert holding a hawk with the sun on its head. I ditched him and went to an alley to meet a woman who would put me in contact with the lady I imagine is now with me at *The Sphinx*. I recollect how cryptic she'd been and didn't expect she could satisfy me, despite her advertised skills in magic. However, to my surprise, but only after we'd performed various unspeakable rites, she had managed to secure a rendezvous with my former wife at an apartment near the Great Gallery.

The dark-haired beauty who greeted me opened a coffin-sized chest painted with colorful glyphs. The interior was filled with vulture eggs amidst writhing snakes and scarabs; but they didn't appear real—the inside of the coffin seemed two dimensional and yet incredibly distant. I told her, "You've been spending too much time alone." I remember how, in preparation for our lovemaking, her closing the heavy curtains was like the movement of broad black wings. But sex didn't happen, as I wasn't sure she was who she said she was. And there were these chilling lamentations coming from another room. As a test, I asked if she still had the ring I'd given her. When she didn't know what I was talking about, my suspicions were confirmed; so, incognito, I fled that phony oasis, finally making it to a port, where I stowed away on a barge bound for Crete. That was decades ago.

We are on our second round of steaming drinks at *The Sphinx* when a catastrophe strikes. Someone has set off a bomb! Fire quickly spreads through the ancient inn and adjoining buildings. I suspect my ex-wife. Large men, ugly as crocodiles, clear everyone out into the street, except for the woman I'd been with, who has disappeared in the smoke and confusion. I tell these men she is of royal blood and must be rescued. I then see the blur of a woman rush into the burning building, so I follow her back into the flames. The woman I love is sitting serenely on the floor waiting to die. "I am prepared," she says dramatically. The shadowy woman tells her she must flee, but the Royal One refuses, explaining she is ready to die because her beloved cats have died, as well as her Great Love. She bids us flee the fire, saying as we rise to go, "The calling forth *is* the fire." We dash outside just as the building collapses with a horrible groan. They never recover her body, and I am stricken with unendurable pain in my soul.

After this incident, curiosity aroused, I initiate an investigation, only to uncover a plot to assassinate me! I imagine the brother of one of the two women is behind it. I'm chased from city to city, across continents, down thousands of winding streets, endless labyrinths, blind curves, dead ends, the unnamed, unknown roads of many foreign lands. Finally, realizing it would be wise to avoid cities, I set off into the jungle. After a fierce struggle through clinging vegetation, I come upon a wide meandering river. Hearing voices, I dive into the brush, then crawl down a twisting "ribbed" tunnel opening onto a grassy clearing. One of the women finds me resting there, in the shade of a flowering magnolia. She assures me of her protection.

We leave the clearing and move into the forest, suffused by a liquid green light, like underwater. Halting for breath, I spot a tiger, its glaring eyes inside a shadow. It roars and charges. I turn to run, but the woman yells, "Wait! It's one of my children." Thus, I discover she didn't die in the flames at *The Sphinx*. Then, walking on two feet, an immense lioness approaches, wearing a crown of fire. I'm terrified, but she says, "There's no danger. Not as long as you are *Remembered*." She hands me a bowl of dates with an asp coiled on top, saying with a fanged grin, "Help yourself." Without hesitation I snatch and eat a date, and feel restored.

Distracted by the lioness, I hadn't noticed a terribly ugly woman with warts and scabs on her face now standing where my lady had been. She's in foul rags; her body covered with oozing sores; hair straggly and dirty; smelling of shit and piss—a witch! I plunge into the dark, cold river, like diving into the night sky. The horrible witch rises up from below and tightly wraps me with her scrawny arms and legs. She hisses she's lost her youth and wants me to return it. I don't understand, but force myself to kiss her disgusting toothless mouth in an attempt to calm her rage. Then another, a faceless woman, is there embracing us both with powerful, yet loving, energy, simultaneously kissing us in a three-way kiss.

We are now up to our waists in a shallow swamp where the water is warm and coagulating. As tiny fish nibble my leg hairs, I spontaneously laugh, suddenly giddy. Their arms and legs locked around me, I see these two are not women after all, but an octopus! Fighting from its deathly grasp, I thrash out of the soupy water and sprint off, alone and exhausted, back through the tangled jungle, up the ribbed tunnel, skirt along the desert's edge, finally return at last into the confounding maze of the City.

Contemplating that I am no closer to knowing which of the two women to choose, or even one from the other, I find myself at attention in a worshipful pose before my girlfriend's house. Lifting my hand, I see I'm holding an orchid corsage in a clear plastic box, and am wearing a tuxedo. Now I remember! It's Prom Night! I gulp, take a deep breath, walk up and ring the doorbell beneath an amber light.

Later, I'm strolling with a black-haired woman. It is still and quiet, house lights out, everyone gone to bed, save for a dog yipping as we pass. Arms around each other, we slowly make our way down the sidewalk of a suburban street lined with maples and elms. It is a balmy spring night, almost tropical. I inhale a mélange of sweet, exotic scents on the warm air. Suddenly I stop, thinking it couldn't possibly be late at night—her hair suddenly turned a brilliant gold, like blonde hair struck by the sun. I tell her this, that her hair just flashed a bright yellow. She peers shyly at me, smiles, and says in a melodious, mature tone of voice for one so young, "The calling forth *is* the fire, my Love."

THE BLUE DEER

A YOUNG MAN WANDERS
through a dark, dense forest of redwoods, giant ferns, rhododendron, dangling orchids, butterflies everywhere splashes of color in the gloom. After bursting through thick brush, he finds himself precariously out on a rock promontory above the silvery pool of a river winding below. Peering over, he notices a deer, just visible in the tree line of dappled sunlight and shade. Without antlers it's perhaps a doe, and bright blue!

He almost topples off the cliff, startled by a looming figure suddenly beside him—a hulking, hideously ugly, mountain man, draped with foul-smelling animal hides, fur cap on a shaggy head; more beast than man, and carrying a long-barreled rifle—who growls he's "gonna to kill that critter."

The young man must prevent this, so he snatches a stick and waves it threateningly, ready to strike. But the brute merely edges closer and glares at him with mean eyes. Glancing back down, the man notices the deer has stepped to the river, maybe to drink. Instead, it dives headlong into the deep pool without making a splash, undulates through the clear water and, in a flash, pops up on the far side, leaping to the safety of the trees. In that blurred moment, the man not only distinctly saw the deer's shiny blue coat, but an image lingers of it darting through the pool as a radiant, orange-streaked, rainbow trout!

Relieved the deer had moved swiftly before the ogre could shoot, the man smiles, and sighs, feeling good he'd distracted the other from firing. Hearing a loud grunt, he whirls around, and is stunned by a wide, blood-shot eye sighting at him down the barrel of a musket. Yet, in that instant, eyeball to eyeball, the two of them recognize each other—they're brothers! With laughter and a dancing hug, they realize the scene just enacted was but another dream.

Leaning out together over the precipice, they stare down at the glowing blue deer, perched on a rock amidst swirling water. Sunlight glitters off rippling wavelets like exploding fireworks. From their roost, they hear the deer laugh too—its high-pitched twitter like a hawk's— and now looking very much like their mother, in her famous blue satin gown, calling them home from play.

THE WAY OF DREAM

A HULKING MAN HAS BROKEN into the house, I don't know how, as everything was locked; but investigating a groan in the front room, I encounter him, standing huge and motionless before me. Despite the dim light, I can see he has skin of burnished copper, a large broad nose, heavy jaw, and shoulder-length black hair that glistens like obsidian. His denim shirt is patched with cloth of many colors, his jeans threadbare, and boots caked with dirt, as if he'd traveled a great distance on foot. Causing my hair to stand on end, he suddenly lifts both fists before him, thumps his chest, and bellows, "I have come from the Old Ones!"

I turn and dash into the bedroom, shut and lock the door, grab my hunting knife to defend myself. But, incredibly, he squeezes right through the door! Fearing for my life, I stab him in the stomach with all my might, holding the knife with both hands, then shove his surprisingly weightless body outside into the cold starry night.

After quickly slamming the door, leaning against it, and breathing hard, I hear his deep voice boom from the outer darkness, "What am I to do now!? You must help me know what to do!?"

NEVER FAR AWAY

I'M BEING QUESTIONED IN A military office across a battered desk by a loud oafish man with a thick neck and severe crew-cut, and sweating through a rumpled slept-in suit. Gazing out the window I am momentarily blinded by rows of gleaming aluminum coffins stacked in the sun. A boy on a cyclo putters by with a woman on back in a blue silk *ao dai*. I'm saddened to see her face has been burned and disfigured. My interrogator shouts, "I didn't get to be Chief by tolerating *clowns* like you!" With forced calm, I respond, "I'm innocent, and have nothing to hide." He towers over me in a threatening way. Sure he'll strike, I recoil, slumping down. I then notice bloody footprints leading into an adjacent room, a kitchen area. Although frightened by him, this bully doesn't appear to be a real threat. So I say, "Could you please explain the phrase *friendly fire*." He turns red in the face, bangs the desk, and glowers like a cartoon bad guy.

Hearing a snicker, I glance into the other room and am shocked to see a childhood pal of mine! Someone had told me he'd been killed in Vietnam. But here he is, sitting placidly in a chair, arms folded across his chest, watching my interrogation with a sly grin. Next to him is a water cooler filled with bubbling red liquid that looks like blood. As if reading my mind, he yells over, "Not to worry, it isn't blood, it's Agent Orange kool-aid!" Then he laughs maniacally, like the exaggerated, theatrical madness in B-horror films.

Rising from his seat my old pal saunters over. Sidling near, he slips some pills into my hand. I completely ignore the inquisitor, still fuming and spitting, to bluntly ask, "What are these?" He just shakes his head.

I loudly whisper, "I won't take them if you don't tell me what they are." Turning away, he acts like he hasn't heard me. He then orders the Chief to leave the room. I am surprised at this, not imagining my crazy friend would be in charge. When we're alone he sets a plastic bag full of multi-colored pills, along with a syringe and a bent spoon, on the table and smirks in that gap-toothed way I remember well from those times in grade school when we got into trouble together.

Closer under the light, I notice he has a badly broken nose and a jagged red scar from the middle of his forehead down around to his chin. He calls me "Specialist" in an ironic manner, demanding I help him wash and wax his custom Chevy. "OK, OK," I say, "but I'll have to change." "Doesn't matter," he chuckles, "these pills will alter every-thing." So we each take a handful of mixed pills, washed down with a few slugs of whiskey, finished off with a toke of opium from a pipe he's lit. "Good shit, huh, man," he wheezes. Nodding automatically, my head bursting with white light, I recall that day long ago, in our secret bamboo-cave hide-out, when we became blood brothers, slicing thumbs and mingling our blood, a bond forever.

My "brother" then hands me a rifle, an M-16, and I know this is mine, the very one I'd carried in Nam. He has one also, along with having put on a bandolier of grenades, an ammo belt and a helmet. Shoving a steel pot onto my head, we step outside, into a night-turned-day by popping illumination flares, streams of red tracer rounds from huey gunships clattering overhead, Phantom air strikes spewing napalm across the horizon … Through this raging, exploding din, he shouts in my ear, "Great to be back, ain't it!"

THE BLADE

"He knows that the dead man is illusory, the same as the bloody sword weighing
in his hand and himself and all his past life and the vast gods and the universe."
—BORGES

$\mathcal{A}$ MAN WHO CALLS HIMSELF
Borges seeks to avenge a murdered friend, killed in a knife fight over a
passionate young woman named Dolores. He takes a dead dog and
carries it to the mountains where he meets a stranger who tells him he
knows him well. Borges disagrees, saying, "The dead dog will need a
dead rabbit." The other man replies, "I can help." Burying the dog at the
mouth of a cave they walk off into the desert until the light grows dim,
and the man named Borges can no longer see. He says to the stranger,
"Dim is a beautiful word, is it not?" But the other is no longer there.
Instead, a tiger pads softly in the sand beside the man known as Borges.

About this time, having been initiated into a secret sword society, I am
told my first assignment is to retrieve the blade from a dying master, and
return with it. In attempting to do this it is necessary for me to kill a
number of worthless men, including one hot-blooded fellow who'd
stabbed a man in the heart in a struggle over a beautiful young lady.

While crossing the desert east of the ruined capital I come across a
blind old man wandering aimlessly in circles beneath the noon sun. He's
speaking in a soft, calm voice, reciting a poem, a saga I recognize from
the Northern epics. Putting my hand on his chest, I stop him and ask,
"Old man, who are you?" He looks at me like I'd disturbed a pleasant
dream, then slowly replies, "I do not know. I've been here so long, longer
than time itself, it seems. But it no longer matters. If it ever did."

Noticing the old man's shadow is that of a large cat, I immediately draw my sword and plunge it through his heart. Later, gathering up his few belongings, a couple slim volumes of stories and poetry, no more, I discover a dagger secreted inside a book. Having completed my mission, I return with his knife in my belt, but not before bleeding a rabbit over the entrance to the sacred cave, saying a prayer for Dolores, now wrinkled and gray, and the men who died because of their love for her.

THE FIRST PEOPLE

I WAS BORN BESIDE A FOUNTAIN in the downtown plaza. Policemen on rooftops were at siesta and thus my birth went unnoticed. My father was slouched outside the cantina, nonchalantly sipping a bottle of red soda, smoking a hand-rolled cigarette. From within the dark bar came music of the Old Land, that country no one alive has seen, but a most real place in stories passed down through the songs. A snare drum, guitars, a violin, clapping hands, stomping feet, the piercing wail of a woman in pain, echoed around the town square.

After my birth I was plucked from the fountain's edge by the hunch-backed street cleaner and placed on a handcart pulled by a withered black man, who spat on me for good luck where I lay in the straw. He hauled me away from that town, from the mother who left me there in the plaza, and the father who said nothing.

I grew up in another province, over the mountains, raised by an old dwarf and his miniature wife. He was the town's mortician, and when I became of age, he taught me an important aspect of his trade: How to properly prepare the heads of the dead, separated from their bodies for special burial. I worked in a cellar with flaking paintings of the first people on its walls, whose eyes followed my labors with intense interest. My labors ... for many years—wrapping the heads with rags soaked in a mixture of plaster, resins, and perfume oils; then I'd set precious stones, turquoise and lapis, into the moist wrappings. When dry I'd put them in a leather box for safekeeping until placed in a nest of other heads in a deep cave on the side of the forbidden mountain. It took me days by burro to get up there. On that mountain I saw many strange and unbelievable things.

But one day in the marketplace my life changed—I found a book filled with colorful maps, magic signs, tales and illustrations of remarkable discoveries and inventions. Learning to read and how to use this book removed the veil from my eyes, giving me insight and courage to leave that village and return to the one of my birth. So, I bid my tearful guardians good-bye and rode out on my burro, over the mountains towards the sea, towards I knew-not-what.

Finally returning to my home town, nestled in hills above the ocean, I immediately locate my father in front of the cantina, sipping a cherry soda, listening with eyes closed to music playing in the dark room behind him. He is not surprised at my arrival, saying he recognized me as soon as I had entered the plaza. Without further explanation, he leads me into the bar, where he indicates a photograph hanging on a wall, a picture of a nursery filled with babies. Then we're inside it! And I'm standing beside the crib of a white-bearded, wrinkled old fellow my father says is his mother's father's father. He then points at two babies in one crib, telling me they are my brother and sister. "They're the shining ones," he adds.

I ask him, "Where's my mother?" He nods out a window. She's alone, sitting stiffly on a stone bench in the shade of a willow as if posing for a picture. She's young and beautiful, and is smiling, obviously content. She wears a new dress, new shoes, make up, and has had her hair styled. I am overjoyed to see my mother and excitedly wave, but she doesn't seem to notice and looks away.

Just then an extremely aged woman, tiny like my guardian mother, hobbles into the nursery. She's bent and shrunken, with white hair hanging down over her robe of rainbow designs and many colors. She appears as ancient as the Earth itself. Clearing her throat, she rasps, "Good, you've come. The first people have been concerned." Then I notice them, glowing and flickering around her like human-shaped flames. I reverently bow, but can't tell if they respond or even see me, their images are so faint and wavering. Then they're gone.

Over in a corner I spy a trunk painted with simplified animals in pastel colors, as in a child's room, and discover it's filled with toys! My eyes widen and I laugh reaching down to remove a stuffed bear, but a claw-like hand slams the lid. The old crone cackles, "Not yet. You're not ready. You have far to go."

Back outside in the glare of day, I leave my father leaning with one foot up against the white plastered wall of the bar, straw fedora pulled down to shield his eyes from the afternoon sun. He has a red soda in one hand and a hand-rolled cigarette in the other. We nod silent good-byes to each other. Turning to walk out of town, I halt beside the fountain, hearing music from the cantina echo around the plaza, but also from everywhere at once, out of every house around the square, sounding down from the distant mountains—guitars, ecstatic shouts, drums, stomping feet, a muted trumpet, the anguished wail of a woman in pain.

AT THE MALL

*I*T'S A SATURDAY, WITHOUT MUCH to do, so I drive to the mall. A shop I hadn't noticed before has the word *Zen* painted on its window in sweeping brush strokes. I go in. A woman in a black robe is sitting on a round cushion in the middle of a shining hardwood floor of an otherwise empty room. I explain to her I'm "stressed out" and need to find my balance. Without a word, she stands, hooks an arm through mine, leads me into a back room, then guides me into a barber's chair, saying, as she shakes out the cloth, "First a light trim. Then food."

After a brief haircut, in which she didn't seem to cut my hair any shorter, we enter a kitchen where she starts preparing a meal. I say, "Is this a joke? Where's the *zen*?" She just laughs in such a spontaneous, childish way I have to laugh along with her. After we eat a delicious sweet potato pie, she says she'll quiz me now. As she begins speaking, I'm amazed to see her levitating! but pretend not to notice.

Her first question is, "If imagination's a window, why does no light pass through?" Without hesitation I reply, "Invisibility's an opaque thought. A blue sphinx." She tosses a glass of water at me. But the glass is empty, and I do not blink. She says, "OK, wise guy. If you're such a survival expert, why were you born?" I put a butter knife between my teeth and walk out.

In the next room I encounter a naked man, who points to another naked man on his back on a table, and on fire! Not burning up really, but covered with small orange flames that flicker over the surface of his body. The first man circles the man on fire, passing his hands through the flames in a stylized way, indicating the ritual is as essential here as the burning man. He says, "This is you." I nod. He comes over, kisses me, then hands me a Tarot card, the four of swords—a knight reclined on a tomb in an attitude of meditative repose. I tell him, "I can't *see*." He says, "There's nothing to see, nothing to do. Be like the man on fire— wear your soul lightly."

Returning out into the mall, I buy an ice cream cone, sit on a bench in the sun, calmly watch people move back and forth, in this ocean of fire.

VOYAGERS

WE ARE CRUISING IN A TWIN-PROP plane returning from a trek through the highest mountains in the world, when ice on the wings causes us to lose altitude, and go into a tailspin. We plough through rocks and snow, eventually coming to a screeching stop against a stone wall. Incredibly, no one is hurt. I extricate myself from the mangled wreck to be greeted by a festive party in progress! We are rushed along by a dancing, laughing, singing crowd into a tent city to view a mimed performance accompanied by flashing lights and clanging music. The actors wear exotic bird costumes of iridescent plumage, silk streamers, and wriggling threads of light. We are informed the story is about an Ancient Being who periodically renews the Known World from Unknown Stuff. This Being appears in the play as a giant vulture.

One swirling apparition asks me to help design a "floating skull" for a concluding episode of the performance. The skull functions as a "holographic key," and is apparently a means of passage into other dimensions. I agree to assist, but only when convinced we're not talking about *my* skull. Later, I wander into a tent with a phosphorescent zodiac glowing on its walls. My sister is there with dad, both standing silently, staring at their feet. Father has white flames around his mouth like pieces of tissue. I try to brush them off but can't. He looks haggard, with bloodshot, squinty eyes. I ask him to pick me up and crack my back, the way he used to do, but he says, "No. I'm not able to touch anything here."

I find my wife by herself sipping a martini. She corrects me, saying, "It isn't a martini, it's an Iced Bardo." When the festivities conclude, we depart on a pilgrimage with our new friends, rumbling along in a stifling, crowded bus. We are stopped at one point by a grotesque battle on the road between strange creatures—gigantic, two-headed chickens versus pigs with eight legs and green faces. These and others look to be mutant farm animals, or freaks of nature. Perhaps the result of nuclear fall-out, or cloning experiments? No one can or will tell us.

During the trip, I'm handed a note saying "a cipher" is chasing us and that I'm on a "mission of essence." After much hard travel we finally reach a magnificent hotel, grand as Versailles. We attempt to elude our mysterious pursuers, but can't flee as my rented chariot has been sabotaged by some inscrutable force. My wife solemnly intones, "The *demons* are onto us." In the lobby I encounter a seedy troll in a filthy pin-striped suit, who wants my help stealing jewels from tourists. He explains in a faux Russian accent that when he throws his toothpick on the ground, if it points one way it means we'll get diamonds, if it points another it means gold. I want nothing to do with his scam, refusing to be coerced by toothpick magic. "Anyway," I say, "I must be going!" He shrugs, and slouches off, spitting splinters.

We sneak off into the surrounding forest, only to discover our "safe house" has been ransacked. I search through the rubble, happy to recover my Boy Scout knife. A mannish gorilla like Bigfoot clomps up out of the trees. Sheepishly, I hand him my knife, but don't understand why as he is scary and menacing. He takes the knife, looks it over, gives it back with a frown, then stomps away shaking his head. Forging on into a meadow of wild flowers we are ambushed by aboriginals with sharp bones and feathers sticking out of their bodies. They shoot turds at us with slingshots and hurl crude spears, the "points" of which are small furry animals. We run away, ducking and dodging their inept attack, until we're on the streets of a quaint village. I lose my wife in a screaming crowd at a tuba concert, so take off by myself to hide in a thatched cottage, where I dive under the bed.

When the excitement dies down, I stroll into the front room where a pensive group of elderly ladies are sipping tea. Suddenly, a leopard crawls out from under the couch and clamps its jaws on my wrist! My heart leaps into my throat. The ladies edge towards me, but I caution them, saying, "Please, don't move" while slowly extricating my arm from the fanged mouth. When the leopard seems distracted, I scoot outside to cool down. Sitting on the grass, I'm inside a circle of beautiful women, who love and adore me! and take turns fervently hugging and kissing me. I recognize them from past voyages, and detect my wife amongst them. We have a long cinematic kiss before a breathtaking sunset, as tubas oompah.

Later, alone, I'm attracted to a fragrant plant with colorful bird-shaped flowers. I stare in awe, thinking, I could paint this, create a masterpiece! Then I focus on some bugs on its leaves that look like tiny white skulls. One takes off towards me, becoming monstrous the closer it gets. It has a wicked-looking stinger, big as a syringe! I run back inside, to find a poetry reading happening. A hushed group waits expectantly in rows of folding chairs before an empty podium. I take a seat beside a man wrapped in bandages. He tells me John Keats will be next. I say, "That's not possible, he's long dead." Another man, looking quite ashen, loudly whispers, "No, not Keats—Kerouac!" I respond, "Well, OK, but he's dead too!"

THE GLYPH OF COMPLETION

*P*ETTING A MAGNIFICENT BLACK cat he's found on the steps to his house, a man is rocked by a stunning woman in a clinging silk dress, hair the same black sheen as the cat's, who approaches, smiles seductively and invites him to a party. He, not having anything better to do on a Saturday night, accepts. The party turns out to be a raucous celebration in a huge house nearby that resembles the Globe Theater. The man wonders how he'd never noticed it before. Nor heard any of the loud party.

Everyone's drinking champagne, singing and yelling at the tops of their voices, dancing, tossing confetti, blowing horns, making love on couches and rugs. He wonders, could it be New Year's Eve? today is midsummer. Having lost his beautiful guide, he looks around for someone he might know, when an extremely drunk, naked woman hands him a small pink pig, saying, "If you sing a number, the pig'll do *anything*." He croons, *twenty-twoooo*, while scratching its nose. The pig, in obvious ecstasy, gives him a silly, loving look, practically human. He quickly hands the pig back to the swaying woman and wanders off.

After numerous similar adventures with many more strange people, he finally encounters the first woman again and offers to take her home, realizing he'd better make his move before getting too drunk. To his amazement she agrees. Leaving the party they embrace in the elevator as it's going down way too fast, like a stone dropped in water. Then they rise again like a bubble. She whispers in his ear in a sexy voice, slipping her hand down his pants, "This is called *The Lion is Loose in the Streets*." He gives a nervous laugh, starting to think he may be in over his head.

At her apartment, she explains she's going to initiate him in *Taming the Lion*. He says, "Right. OK. Does it hurt?" She giggles, meanwhile disrobing them both in a twinkling of an eye, then exclaims, "It's showtime!" And it certainly was.

Next morning she tells him they not only *Tamed the Lion*, but also *Induced The Clever Trance*, *Collated the Opposites*, *Rode the Orgasmo-Go-Round*, did *The Ritual Unbuttoning of the Navel*, and formed *The Glyph of Completion*. He admits it was a learning experience. As she takes him to the door and they kiss, she transfers some "bliss gum" from her mouth to his. He chews it night and day.

SNAKE STEW

I'M IN THE BACKYARD WITH my mother. She points to an old chicken coop with large nests in it made by wild animals. She wants the whole thing removed. I say all right and begin dismantling the shed. The nests contain balls of dung that are smooth, hard, and of various colors like billiard balls. I wipe off these unusual objects and place them neatly in a cardboard box to present to my teacher.

Upon arriving home earlier, I'd brought mother a burlap sack of a variety of snakes I'd captured for her to make into a stew. After disposing of the chicken coop I start chopping up the snakes on a tree stump using my scout hatchet. Amazingly, one of the snakes, a red-and-green-striped one, is still alive, even after being cut into pieces. It slithers off, reunited and unharmed, into the deep grass. Mother yells out through the screen door she doesn't like the idea of snake stew. Unfazed, I continue chopping the serpents into bite-sized chunks. Then, noticing mother drive off with a man I don't recognize, I decide to make stew at my teacher's house.

My guru has a long curly beard, silver hair, and skin so jet black it is difficult to discern features. His face shimmers like a pool of crude oil. We rarely exchange words. This puzzles me, as I'm usually bursting with a million questions to ask, but never do. Arriving, I find him out back in lotus position beneath a laurel tree, the one he calls "Old Slumber." I silently hand him the box of colorful dung along with the sack of snake bits. After peering and sniffing into each, he looks up at me with the leering face of a fox, which astonishingly changes into a hawk, then into the snarling face of a tiger. I climb up into the tree in a hurry.

Saucer-eyed, I am staring down at a huge gray wolf looking back up with piercing yellow eyes, eyes that shoot laser beams right through me. The wolf has a red-and-green snake writhing in its jaws, yet stares at me with such an inquisitive, friendly look. But as I'm not too sure about that, I stay put. Later, at sunset, I cautiously climb down, make my way through the darkening yard, run home, and enter the house. Mother is in the kitchen in front of the stove basting a skinned rabbit. Looking up, she gives me a tender smile. Her eyes are bright gold. I take my seat at the dining table with the others, fold my hands, wait quietly for dinner.

GREEN

*A*FTER A STRENUOUS CLIMB up a rocky cliff a man finally enters a cave he'd spotted through binoculars from the beach below. His companion, a woman, catches up within moments. Pulling herself over the lip of the cave, out of breath, she gasps, "Gosh! What beautiful statues! They're green!" The man, dumbstruck, points to a wall of pure, polished malachite, then approaches it, as if in a trance, to trace its green marbled swirls with his finger. Despite darkness in the cave, its green walls emit a soft glowing illumination, allowing them to see the stone objects clearly. Regaining his voice, he excitedly tells her, "I'll get out my hammer and chisel! We'll carve statues of ourselves! If it's too hard we'll alter them to our likenesses."

They notice many carvings have already been vandalized, some defaced, others completely wrecked. With much effort, boosting and pulling each other, using a leaning statue as a ladder, they crawl up onto a tall malachite pedestal at the center of the cavern. Not able to resist an impulse, he kicks over the statue propped against their perch. Although badly mutilated, he can see the figure is part-human, part-something else, perhaps a lion, maybe a bear. It crashes into pieces amongst the debris on the floor, sending up a cloud of fine dust that causes them to choke.

With rising tension in her voice, the woman shouts between coughing fits, "Why did you do that!?" She's apprehensive for the first time since they'd entered the cave. He merely responds with an air of studied authority, "We must clean the slate if we are to transform ourselves. Understand?" "Are these statues of gods?" she wonders. "Of course," he says, "but these gods are old and dead. So now it's our turn.

Let's go to work!"

But upon attempting to climb down from the pedestal they discover they cannot—when he'd pushed over the statue their means to descend was removed. The pillar is too high to jump from without breaking ankles on the stone fragments below, and too smooth to allow a foothold without sliding down in an equally perilous way. They appear to be stuck. Suddenly it's freezing cold inside the cave. They hug each other, trembling atop the glowing pedestal, inside a swirling storm of green light, and clinging shadows.

IN THE OLD COUNTRY

*I*N THE OLD COUNTRY EVERYONE
is poor and anemic. A man gets in line to buy gruel and maybe a
scrawny bird, if he's lucky. At the front he orders a smoked sparrow but
receives a slice of cardboard instead. Disappointed, he asks how much
for a clove of garlic. The grocer says, "One Gee." The man hands over a
poker chip. The grocer barks, "This won't do." "Sorry," says the man,
"it's what I have." Hungry, he trudges home to his hovel near the
factory, where he must hide his bedclothes each morning in fear
someone will break in and steal them.

On the way he meets a policeman who snarls, "I hope the hole you're
standing in has nothing to do with *revolution*!" Then orders the man to
dispose of a body nearby, strutting off in a Napoleonic manner, patent-
leather boots gleaming. The man looks around, loses sight of the body,
but finds it sitting up against a mailbox like waiting for a letter. "This is
no good," he mutters. "Too near the road." He hauls the body to an
empty lot, but it is too close to the palace. Finally, after rejecting
numerous places, he decides on a spot deep in the woods and drags the
body up the side of a cliff, where, despite being on a high ledge in the
dark, he digs a grave. Making a hole, he sticks his head inside, only to
see he's broken into a room.

He runs to find the policeman to say he's gone through the wall of a
room and would he come unlock the door leading into it from the other
side. "That's a hermit's cave," the cop hisses, "and no way to bury a
body!" He then takes a golden egg from his holster and flips it in the air.
The man catches it in his hat. Putting the hat on his head cracks the egg,

which runs down his face. The policeman laughs, gives him a metal box with coiled wires sticking out, explaining it works like a geiger counter.

The man returns to the hole and squeezes into the room. It is small and sparsely furnished, reminding him of his own. The ticking box gets louder and louder. He pulls open the cobwebby door. There's a vampire in a silk cape lying across the threshold. Although the creature is ghastly looking, the man isn't afraid—merely curious as to what will happen, as he carefully sets the box on its chest. The vampire sits upright and begins speaking intensely, as if continuing an unbroken conversation: He claims he is *eternal*, and says many other things very fast in a mock-serious tone of voice.

Not forgetting his assignment, the man buries himself instead.

REALITY

$\mathcal{G}$RANDMOTHER LIVES IN A battered, antique house trailer at the end of a torturous dirt road out in the desert, miles from the main highway. Her nearest neighbor is a rarely seen ex-husband who inhabits a shack on the opposite side of the arroyo. As I approach on foot, slapping dust off my pants, I see her peering out a curtained window through those thick glasses that magnify her eyes to enormous size. This always spooked me as a child. I'm no less spooked now.

After kissing a sandpaper-coarse cheek, right off I show her a tattered fatigue jacket and launch into the tale of how it was once owned by a buddy of mine killed in the war by a sniper. And how he'd been standing not ten feet away with some papers in his hand, then just toppled over, dead—a perfect shot right through the heart. I tell grandmother I want her to make a hat for me from this special jacket I'd worn through my many journeys, now ragged and useless as a coat.

After I finish my breathless story, she snatches the jacket from my hand and tosses it into a fire smoldering in a brazier. The coat ignites with a bright hissing flash like gunpowder. Then she digs into a steamer trunk and pulls out a strange floppy black hat, looking like a dead crow; but reaching for it I hesitate—seeing a living thing, a pulsating piece of darkest night floating mid air between us …

Squatting at the jungle's edge, my glazed eyes stare out at a rice paddy and a wall of more dense jungle beyond, at bright dawnlight sparkling off neat rows of blue water, at a lone water buffalo knee-deep in mud, immersed in the complete stillness of the moment. Then a great stream of light rushes towards me! ... and the water buffalo explodes.

This is real, I tell grandmother. Yes, yes, she says, presenting me with my new hat. Yes it is.

VIGIL

*I*N A CHAPEL MADE OF GLASS and perfectly-fitted granite blocks, like Machu Picchu, I'm at a desk in the sun of a bay window jotting down words I remember said by my father. I'm trying to capture his Philosophy of Life, but can recall only a single phrase: "Take your inner self," he'd said, "and wrap it around the outer self." Perhaps that's enough, I note.

A movement outside catches my eye—looking into a garden, I'm surprised to see dad out there! Wearing coveralls, his old fishing hat with all those lures hooked on it, he's holding his sides, laughing. Fat silver tears roll down his pink cheeks.

Noticing me, he glides over to the window and peers in, as if squinting into watery depths; then he shouts, "Someone up on the road called me *fool!*" Thinking this terrifically funny, he laughs uproariously again, shaking his head like "I can't believe it." With a conspiratorial wink and a big grin, he turns and bounces away through rows of nodding roses, taking great weightless bounds like on the moon, until he vanishes over a green knoll dotted with dandelions.

Charmed, I get up from the desk, cross the room and sit down at a pipe organ to play. Although I don't know how, I *do* play—a requiem mass by Bach, but in stuttered "spacious" tempo of Thelonious Monk. And this feels great!

Distracted by voices, I go over to the sacristy, where a group of elders dressed head to toe in black are in straight-backed chairs formed in a semi-circle. They are quiet and still, but glance over abruptly when aware of my presence in their sanctuary. I wonder out loud if the dirge

I'd just played was satisfactory? After looking at each other with mute questioning, they then give me identical expressions of profound puzzlement. Finally, one old fellow breaks the spell, demanding, "Who *are* you!?" Cheerfully I reply, "The Son of the Fool, of course!" Then giggle.

For some minutes, these ancient folk continue to stare up at me with silent, owl-eyed astonishment; and I do the same in turn, watching amazed, as they slowly dim and fade from sight. Back at the desk, I collect my notebook, write: "And laughter."

SOME GREAT SECRET

*B*ECAUSE I'VE GOTTEN LOST ON an unfamiliar country road at night, I decide to pull over and sleep in the car until morning, when I'll feel fresher and can better see where I'm going. After quickly dozing off, a rattling noise wakes me at what I guess to be very late, as the moon has moved across the sky. I sit up immediately.

Without city lights nearby, a crescent moon and stars offer my only light. Yet I can make out something hanging from the partially rolled-up window, and reflexively brush it off, like swatting at a bug in front of your face. After doing so, I realize with a shudder of revulsion that the *something* is a pair of small hands!

Holding my breath, I roll down the window, hesitantly peer out, do a "classic" double take—I've knocked down a tiny person! But I can see it's not a *human* person—it has silver reptilian skin, soft features of a baby with tiny, perfect hands and feet, a smooth bald head and shiny transluscent body. This is surely an adult gazing back at me through glittering, ageless, sad eyes, or perhaps sardonic, with a vague, mysterious smile curving its slit of a mouth. The little creature cocks its head, as if curious as to what *I* might be, then stands upright in a single fluid motion, elongating itself directly towards my stricken face. Like grabbing an electric wire, I swoon back in a dead faint.

Awakened by bright daylight, I sneeze many times, like I'd inhaled pepper, then, without looking around, start the engine and roar off. In the rear-view mirror I'm relieved to see nothing but billowing clouds of dust in my wake. After a short distance, I notice a horse grazing near a split-rail fence beside the road. As I drive slowly by, it looks up, and I have the definite impression the animal's reading my mind, or knows something I don't, and is gloating about some great secret.

So I stop the car and get out. Turning in a circle, I realize my entire surroundings are dead silent, not a sound; and there's great pressure on my ears, like in a diving bell falling through the sea, but including these rolling hills, oak trees, herd of cows, farmer on a tractor, a dog sitting in the road—no sounds, anywhere. More astonishingly, nothing moves. Even birds overhead are perfectly still, hanging like props in a stage show. Hungry and alone in this idyllic scene, I bend my long neck down for a nibble of sweet dewy grass, swish my tail at a pesky fly.

DOWN HERE

$\mathcal{M}$ANY OF US HAVE GATHERED in a dimly-lit room of a Spanish-style villa, illuminated only by candles set on the floor. Tapestries cover the walls, there's a Turkish carpet, but no furniture. We are seated on cushions on the rug around an exceedingly fat, brown-skinned woman, who is addressing us. Her voice is melodious and sweet, now sounding like a lark, now a little girl, a bamboo flute, a stream splashing over stones. She is from the East, I'm told, and is divinely beautiful. She has a golden hoop in her nose, tinkling bracelets, gold and silver rings on fingers and toes, a red dot between her eyes. She wears nothing else, yet her nakedness seems not unusual. I am in love with this woman because her stories go *bing! bing! bing!* all over the place, then make perfect sense at the end. We, her devotees, agree she is indeed marvelous. We are in awe, and worship her, allowing whatever mood she's in to touch us deeply.

After her discourse, we listen to recordings of gypsy songs—guitars strum, dogs bark, the singer cries in a language I can only feel. While we raptly listen, the Woman slumps onto her back in a trance; as she does, the copious fat of arms, legs, breasts and belly rolls and sags, making her body quite amorphous, like molten chocolate. Her hair pools around her massive head in a black corona. Her pouting thick lips open and close as if drinking air like a fish. While gaping at her, a man without a face passes me a hashish pipe with two bowls, apparently smoked from the middle. I say, "I know how to do this." However, I smoke it clumsily, choke, and feel foolish. But the others aren't interested in *me*, so it doesn't matter, absorbed as we are in the music and contemplation of the tremendous body of this woman many think of as Mother, now snoring softly, her plasmic form quivering with each breath.

After she awakens and rises, sitting like a great up-welling of living earth, she appears transformed into a powerful and frightening sorceress. She speaks again, this time in a harsh voice like a growling beast, telling us how her children have all died under mysterious circumstances, perhaps murdered by evil ones. Some of us gasp, others sob. Then she relates in a cackling voice a graphically detailed porno-graphic tale about a troupe of carnival freaks who make love in extremely bizarre ways. Many in the group are not only offended by this story but by the ugly change of our Beloved Mother, and quickly leave the room. Standing to do the same, my mind spins and my eyes won't focus—my body's whirling around *within* my body! The Woman's horribly discordant voice only makes it worse.

I manage to grope outside, where my vision clears upon entering a courtyard surrounded by buildings on various levels and with many staircases, arcades, and vanishing points that defy a sense of perspective. No trees or flowers anywhere, it's all brick and stone. There are two naked dark-skinned men, bound and tied to the tops of tall poles amidst a crowd of angry people. I wonder if perhaps this is because of something I've done or failed to do? I slug myself in the solar plexus and double over with a groan.

The mob is preparing to torture one man by putting electric wires to his testicles. I intervene by pointing and shouting at the fat woman, who has rolled outside to oversee the cruel rite. I yell, "I'm sick of your corrupt and manipulative ways!" As the mob disperses, the witch grimaces and snarls, obviously wanting to strike out and kill me, but she cannot. My words seem to have broken a spell of violence and despair, maybe she has induced, whether intentionally or not, I do not know. As she cowers back into the shadows, her laughter bounces around the courtyard, but instead of being grating and terrible, it is humorous and loving again, as if what had just happened is but another playful story, in which we all play our parts.

I help untie the men and lead them back inside the villa. Re-entering the main room I am startled to see *myself* naked on the floor in the middle of a circle of people wearing cloaks and masks of feathers and fur. I overhear one of them, a tiger, whisper to an owl, "If we keep the lights low, he'll never notice." With an intense effort, as if a heavy stone had been placed on my chest, I struggle up and peer into the gloom, blinking my eyes at the phantasmic figures seated around me.

*A*N OLD MAN HAS JOINED ME in the gym to shoot baskets. He has thick curly gray hair and a "walrus" moustache, and is small in stature, but in no way stooped or aged, radiating vitality and liveliness. When it's my turn to shoot, I attempt to impress him doing lay-ups by taking off my cowboy hat at the same time. But neither my hat nor the ball will go through the net for me. I miss everything, shot after shot. So I challenge him to a free-throw contest. He goes first, hits ten in a row, then a few from further out beyond the key. I think he's a magician or has some special powers, and tell others who enter the gym, "Hey! This old guy never misses a shot!" Then we go outside and are talking, leaning up against a car, enjoying the sunshine, when a gang of swaggering punks approaches. I whisper to the old man, "Use your powers to take care of these guys." He replies, "My 'powers,' as you call them, are to be used for *beauty*, not for violence."

Later, I'm by myself at a secluded cabin beneath pines near an alpine lake. It seems I'm there to make it *better*, cleaner, nicer. Inhaling the invigorating scents on the crisp mountain air, I "tightrope" on a log jutting into the clear shallows, where baby trout strike at gnats on the water's surface. The ripples they make expand across the lake and, I imagine, all the way out across the universe.

Back on shore I am utterly alone, and suddenly uneasy. Down along the beach, I notice a big dog or perhaps a wolf loping directly towards me! Frightened, I frantically search for a stick or a rock to use as a weapon. Then, looking back around, the dog or wolf has disappeared, and I am startled by a figure right beside me! It's the same bushy-haired old guy from the gym.

Disconcerted, I blurt out, "I didn't see or hear you because it is so quiet here at this beautiful place and because of the ceaseless noise in my head." It then occurs to me the only way I'll make this place *better* is by distancing myself from that constant chatter in my brain. The old man does not respond. Instead, he does a couple fancy steps sideways, mimes taking a jumpshot, then laughs happily, throwing his hands in the air after swishing a 20-foot shot to win the game at the buzzer.

END OF THE GAME

A NUMBER OF PEOPLE ARE sleeping in a big dormitory in bunk beds and cots, men and women together. A gigantic flying insect buzzes around, rousing us. Someone turns on the lights so we may find out what's disturbed our sleep. Wide awake now, I see a miniature frog-boy riding a dragonfly, clinging to its gossamer wings, waving and smiling at me like a long-lost friend! I avert my eyes, hoping none of the others noticed. But they are oblivious and have wandered into the living room. I decide it best to ignore it as well, and join them.

We take our seats at a round table and begin the game. Soon I'm playing footsie with a voluptuous woman beside me, and surreptitiously open my bathrobe to show her I have an erection. She titters, blinking eyes and covering her mouth, pretending to be shocked, then hisses, "Concentrate on the game!" I try. We attempt to explain to one man, who's always been a wise guy, that he must choose a concrete *thing*, not an abstraction like *sublimation*. He doesn't get the concept of the game. We heckle him until he begrudgingly chooses *tomahawk*—and in 1847 a dry goods clerk in South Dakota is killed by a guided missile.

Remembering I have a rendezvous down by the river, I excuse myself and dash out into the night. Under the porch light I see the flying insect with the frog-boy has followed me. Still pretending not to see them, I charge across the broad moonlit lawn, through a grove of cottonwoods, to the edge of a smooth-flowing river, where I take my seat on a patch of grass beside a moss-bearded grandfather oak, its roots tenaciously gripping a boulder jutting from the bank. Being early

Spring, the river is high from melting snow, as it rolls quietly along like an immense serpent.

The frog-boy is in my face again, lit up like a lightning bug by an inner fire. And once again I ignore it, as I tear pages from my book of illuminations, watch the white leaves float away on the undulant back of the river. I sit motionless, aware only of my breath rising and falling—riding the dragonfly, hovering amongst the stars, waiting for the game to end.

MANY MANSIONS

*I*ENTER THE PLUSH SITTING ROOM
of a Victorian mansion with high parquet ceilings, marble statues, and
wooden pillars, filled with furniture from many historical periods.
Hearing a cracking noise, I see a bear cub up on a shelf knocking bric-a-
brac onto the floor with much crashing and breaking of crockery. To my
horror, a mama bear lumbers into the room, roars, stands to full frightening height, and roars again, displaying dripping fangs. She drops
onto all fours and charges before I can move. In a flash she's on my back
and bites into my shoulder, her teeth sinking in down to the bone.
However, I feel no pain, nor experience any fear; and don't cry out. I
then surprise myself by caressing the bear's paws and long claws now
wrapped around my ribcage. These are intimate caresses and vaguely
erotic, I sense, for both of us.

Released, I leave the bears and rush up a red carpeted stairway into
mother's bedroom, finding her asleep in a four-poster atop a white lace
bedcover. She's in her old quilted bathrobe, but also has on high heels,
nylons, lipstick and rouge, like she's been out on the town or getting
ready to go out. I softly touch her arm and whisper, "There are bears in
the house!" Then louder, "Mom, wake up! There are bears!" She doesn't
stir. So I gently scoop her up in my arms and carry her downstairs to
show her the bears, now snuffling around in the pantry, tearing open
cupboards, ripping apart cereal boxes and bags of flour. Mom still won't
wake up, and I notice her extreme paleness, her long brown hair falling
out in clumps.

Giving up trying to awaken her, I carry her into the den and lay her down on a leather couch. I walk leadenly into another bedroom where I throw myself onto a bed and immediately fall asleep. Later a tall thin ghostly figure in a white gown appears, staring down at me from the end of the bed. The face of this person is angelic, ethereal, innocent. I attempt to ask, "Who are you?" but only stutter, the words catching in my throat. I then try shouting with greater force and anxiety, "Who are you? Who!?" Whereupon, mother shakes my shoulder, waking me, saying in a breathless, concerned voice, "Dear, this isn't *our* house."

NEVER NAKED

$\mathcal{A}$ MAN ENTERS AN AUDITORIUM where a conference of psychiatrists is taking place. The participants sit attentively on white plastic chairs arranged around a woman's face that shows through a hole in the floor. Pretending to be the Delphic Oracle, she utters deep-voiced cryptic pronouncements to the rapt group of shrinks, wildly scribbling her words onto yellow notepads. The man knows who she really is, but doesn't let on.

Many strange and exotic odors blow through the cavernous hall. The man thinks, "I'll concentrate on just one!" As he does, an ugly oaf with warts on his face and a single big tooth in his mouth frightens him at a burrito stand in Kathmandu. In the next instant, he is aware of the voice of the Oracle whispering in his mind, "There are bugs in your burrito, my dear." He chuckles to himself.

A holy war breaks out in the room. The man finds himself chosen leader of one faction, and announces in a "masterful" voice, "I am never naked!" He is immediately overtaken by heavily armed shadows that congeal into a gooey stinking mass. Summoning all his resources, he rolls this great ball of dung up a steep slope to the Capitol, where a cadre of politicians in gray metallic suits surrender to him with solemn pomp and ceremony.

At a party to celebrate the new era of peace and freedom, someone puts a slow "oldie-but-goodie" on the record player, as the house lights dim. The man dances close, cheek-to-cheek, with the gorgeous Oracle, now wearing a fuzzy pink sweater, tight red skirt, white socks and penny loafers. She is no longer pretending; and the combined sweat and musky teen-age perfume of her sends his senses reeling. When the music changes to a fast number, they do some nifty twirls and spin right on out the doors into the parking lot. Grabbing her hand, he shouts, "Come on! Let's make it to Lover's Lane!" Their escape noticed, they hear pained shrieks from the psychiatrists as they sprint off hand in hand through the bright suburban night, extending into an ever-unpredictable future.

MOUNTAINS

*M*Y BROTHER, SISTER AND I, along with a few friends, are on a hike through orange groves behind our house. I observe a range of snow-capped mountains in the distance, as grand and majestic as the Himalayas. Not having noticed these mountains before, I stare harder wondering if they're real or a summer mirage. But, comparing this incredible sight with my companions, we agree they are indeed *there*, covered with glittering whiteness like rough crystals below a clear blue sky. Deciding to give the mountains a closer look, we set out.

Along the way, our band is joined by a group of very tiny women who've materialized out of the bush. Wearing skirts and blouses of vivid colors in intricate patterns, they appear featureless, except for their colorful attire—I cannot tell what race they might be or even the expressions on their faces, hidden as they are beneath shawls embroidered with stylized designs of plants and animals. These marvelous elfin women move quietly with us like a covey of quail, darting here and there, but always staying close, sometimes too close, as they scoot between legs, causing someone to trip, which initiates loud laughter all around. And no one questions who or what they might be, or why they're even with us, so enthralled are we by their enjoyable antics.

After hiking through walnut and orange groves into progressively thinning woodlands, we arrive onto a bluff overlooking a depressing sight—a chaos of freeways, houses, power lines, factories, office buildings, and shopping malls blocking our path to the wondrous mountains beyond. We must return; there's no way to hike through all *that* in one day, if at all. I say out loud, but mostly to myself, "I'll try this again sometime." As consolation, we decide to take a different route back through the woods. I'm walking ahead on this begrudging return, feeling low, when I spy a hobo camp beneath a bridge spanning a dry wash. This worries me, so I rejoin the others, deciding if there should be any trouble it would be best to stay together.

When I reconnect with the group, I discover the tiny women are missing. My sister is sobbing, and my brother anxiously exclaims, "They're gone!" We begin looking for them at once. From under a pile of garbage I hear shrill voices cry, "Help us! Help us!" I rush over and dig through this mound of trash. As I do, out of the corner of my eye, I glimpse a crusty, gray-bearded man in rags hobble over and squat down on a large flat rock nearby. Intently watching my frantic efforts he mumbles something to me, but as I am trying to rescue the tiny women, I ignore him.

No longer hearing their cries, and after scouring the area, under bushes, roots, behind rocks, the entire dump site and surrounds, we abandon the search as it is growing dark. The tiny ladies have totally vanished. Sad and confused, we all note how colorless and dull the world seems without them. Hearing a strange scraping nearby, I glance back towards the rock where the hobo had been. Instead, there's a mountain lion! sitting back on its haunches, and staring directly at me with calm interest, as if with wondering appraisal.

Beyond the lion, across the gully behind it, I notice my brother and sister jumping up and down, wildly waving their arms. They are shouting, yet I can't make out a word. But, fluttering around their feet— the colorful flock of little women! And I feel glad. Then the lion rises up onto all fours, leans forward like it will pounce, and says close to my face, "Learn all you can about chaos. Then begins the art of dying." I stutter, "Th-thanks," slowly back away, and tear off through the woods, zig-zagging like lightning.

POOL HALL

*E*NTERING A TYPICALLY OBSCURE, drab pool hall, I'm instructed to donate a buck to the stew. I shrug, and throw a dollar into a bubbling kettle tended by a burly tattooed guy with a round unshaven jaw. I peer into the pot. It contains a variety of unrecognizable chunky stuff along with obnoxious odors off its mélange of bizarre ingredients. I think I see fur, tails, teeth, tiny skulls, but refuse to believe my eyes. I ask the cook how the tradition started, of putting money in a stew. Disturbed from his methodical stirring, he shoots a look that reads, how dumb are you?

I get a game and am lining up a shot—a difficult two-banker to graze a ball into a side pocket. My opponent is standing behind me. I ask him to please move, he makes me nervous. This happens a few times, and odd thing is, each time I eyeball a shot the "felt gets greener," like through my *will* alone I'm getting straighter and easier shots. Finally, after running the table, it's a simple poke at the 8 ball. But glancing down I see I'm wearing "Star Wars" pajamas! and peer sheepishly about, wondering if anyone else notices. They don't seem to, so I coolly stroke the shot, sending the cue ball flying off the table to land in the stew pot, splashing its messy contents into the face of the brawny chef. I barely get out of there alive.

Next night I return to the pool hall hoping all's forgiven. I have an overwhelming sensation of being on another planet, induced by watching two guys fight—as one tries to punch the other, the second guy folds over onto the first like closing a suitcase, covers himself with a layer of carrots and explodes into flames! I have this exhilarating feeling Bugs Bunny will pop up next! Instead, the cook, like an angry gorilla, grabs me and demands a game. Knowing better, I tell him I simply *must* finish *Remembrance of Things Past* tonight, or the library will revoke my social calendar. He pouts, responding with a world-weary, "Je comprends."

Strolling home in the dark, whistling to keep werewolves at bay, I think what a wonderful place the pool hall is! like a time machine, a vault of Loony Tunes, and plan to return again—as long as The Force is with me.

MEMORY

$\mathcal{R}$ECOGNIZING THE IMMENSE maple tree in the yard, its heavy branches extending above the wooden house and over the sidewalk, the man approaches a white-haired crone seated in a rocking chair on the front porch. The place is dilapidated now and in a neighborhood he knows he shouldn't be in, as it's become dangerous. *She has replaced my grandmother.* This thought does not seem odd to him. He accepts its strangeness matter-of-factly, saying to the woman, "My grandmother was a good and gracious lady." She agrees with a slight nod and a wrinkled smile, then hands him a plate of warm cookies.

Seated on a step, eating the cookies and drinking a glass of milk, he observes a small boy come down the street, then turn and enter the yard through the broken gate, walk up the weed-lined path and up the creaky steps. On the porch, the boy acts like the man and old woman are invisible as he marches straight past them and calls out through the screen door to someone inside. The man barks, "This isn't your house! You should not be here!" The boy begins to cry; so, feeling bad, the man leads him inside. The boy goes straight to an overstuffed chair, curls up and falls asleep.

The man casually strolls through the familiar house, inspecting various dusty objects, then suddenly rushes out the back door, remembering a friend had been in trouble. Peering into the garage he's relieved to find his old companion is OK after all. Despite the dimness, it's obvious his pal's been cleaned and oiled—it gleams! Entering slowly through the long shadows of early evening into the open garage, he hears it speak, the voice coming from the freshly painted front forks. The black balloon-tire bicycle tells him, "I've been renewed. All is well. No need to worry." The man sees the colorful plastic streamers dangling from the handle grips, missing fenders and chain guard for aerodynamic sleekness, the dinged rear fork when he'd gone into a ditch, baseball cards in the spokes, held with clothes pins. Upon looking closer, he sees each card is a picture of *himself* in an heroic "action pose," playing every position with nobility, excellence, and pride.

He straightens up stiffly in the damp, musty garage reeking of old oil, grease, rotting wood, newspapers, rusted tools. He can smell the aftermath of the fire he'd caused—a chemistry project gone horribly awry. Inhaling deeply with eyes closed, he sees a thousand bright images, scenes of his glory years, the triumphs and defeats, enemies overcome, the lovely maidens—pictures fixed forever in his mind. Patting the bike seat, he says, "So long" and walks out. Behind him echoes a high-pitched, "See ya around!"

Returning to the house, he finds the sleeping boy has gone. The old lady is still out on the porch, quilt over her knees, quietly rocking. When she recognizes him, she beckons him over, eyes smiling, like she's going to tell a great joke. "Whoosh, whoosh," she whispers, "don't tell anyone," as she hands him a shiny silver dollar—a most wonderful thing! As he touches her hard, blue-veined hand, he falls into the endless well of memory, where the tingling cold of the north country stings his face, and fills his lungs.

GAS STATION

*A*T A GAS STATION WITH MY BROTHER, filling the tank of the car. It's night. A homeless-looking man appears in the light and asks if we'd like to see a trick. I shout, "No! Don't do it!" as he takes the nozzle and drinks, thinking he's going to ignite the gasoline. He does spit it out, but without lighting it, as it amazingly pours forth in one long slow-motion stream. To our further astonishment, this jet of gasoline from his mouth transforms into a rainbow of bright sparkling colors that just hangs there, suspended in the space between us.

The guy then grabs both ends of this "rainbow" and pulls and stretches it, the gasoline now jelled into a solid, until the rainbow becomes a grid-like pattern of blinking, multi-colored, overlapping stripes and squares. He then holds this magical piece of art up, displaying it with obvious pleasure and pride in his handiwork. Staring at it, I sense that if the squares would only stop flashing and moving I'd be able to behold pictures. I also have the impression maybe he thinks I *can* see actual images, when, in fact, I do not.

We offer him some money, which he refuses, so we get into the car and drive off. Deeply touched by what I've witnessed, I dumbly ask, "What *was* that gasoline? Who *was* that fellow pulled a rainbow out of his body?" My brother looks over, smiles weirdly, shrugs and says, "Can't blame it on the aliens." I nod in reflection.

Glancing in the rear-view mirror I see a deer, or a man in a deer-skin cape with antlers on his head, step cautiously onto the road from the brightly lit gas station, scuttle across then vanish into the darkness on the other side.

FAMOUS AUTHOR

I TAKE A SLOW TRAIN SOUTH through the great desert to visit a famous author living in a Mexican town, a wearying two-day journey. The streets and shops seem familiar, as if I'd once been here, but I'm sure I haven't. I go to a bar, *Cantina La Higuera*, also the only hotel, and where he lives. Entering its dark cool interior, I recall being here before, absolutely, and am confused— perhaps my memory's failing, or I've stepped into another's life? The desk clerk, an old indian with silver hair, leads me up stairs so poorly lit I must cling to the wall, down an equally dim hallway with a shuttered window at its end, to the writer's room. But it's empty. "Good riddance," grunts the old man, "he was an hombre muy loco." Disappointed, and not knowing what else to do, I take the vacant room. At sunset I go out for food, knowing a good café past the abandoned rail station near the river.

Hurrying through the crumbling brick station, I have to move around and over dark shapes sleeping on the floor. At least, it appears they're sleeping, or passed-out drunk, or worse. The dank place smells of rotten meat. Stepping back outside, I wobble, sensing the possibility of truly slipping into another life. However, I am reassured to find the café. And with thousands of tiny lights still strung on the adobe building and draped in adjacent willows and saguaros. The place is throbbing with raucous party sounds, the people stomping a group dance to lively music from musicians on a balcony. But there are no tables, and no food at this hour. So I leave that noisy scene, wolf down a couple green chile tamales at a stand on the main street, return to the hotel. Prone on the hard bed, I am mesmerized by two greenish-blue lizards on the ceiling circling the bare lightbulb. Drifting off, I hope tomorrow will be less ambiguous, not so "wobbly."

I jerk awake. The light is blinding. The window is black, it must be late. I get up, cautiously creep down the hall, enter an open door into a candle-lit room. An indian with fine handsome features, like a younger version of the desk clerk, is on a bench holding a large book. It has "root-like" women on its cover, like mandrake roots, but definitely female. The title is hard to make out, but is perhaps *Puja*. A woman beside him has long dark hair obscuring her face. Taking a step towards them, he glances up and says in English, but with a strange non-Spanish accent, "You should not continue as you've been, but follow the way of Shakti." He tilts his head towards the woman, who twists her face up towards me like a carp rising from murky depths. Her eyes are a solid milky white, her skin extremely pale, as if never touched by the sun. She doesn't move her lips, yet I hear quite clearly: *Su vida esta solamente una reflexión.* Her voice vibrates like a tuning fork inside my body.

Trembling, I dash into the empty street, and stride briskly out of town far into the desert, where there are no houses, no lights, just the vast dome of blackness arrayed with stars. Leaving the road, I go down into a dry riverbed and enter a grove of fruit trees, where I come upon two women sitting silently beside baskets of tangerines, apples, peaches, and figs. One woman, with dark eyes radiant in the starlight, says forcefully, "I know you." But I don't know her—how could she possibly know me? She says in the same bold manner, "What does *fig* mean?" I notice other people quietly standing and sitting amongst the trees, as if they'd suspended all activity upon my arrival. Holding out a ripe fig split by the sun, she continues in her eerily booming voice, "Does anyone know what *fig* means?" I turn and run back along the riverbed, each footstep crunching through the hard crust of sand. Rounding a bend, I encounter the man from the candle-lit room perched on a rock on the bank. Breathlessly, I ask if he'd please look up *fig* in his book, por favor; but he sits immobile, staring straight ahead, silhouetted by stars. I rush back to town, hearing him call after me, "The Way! Don't forget the Way!"

The rising sun behind me transforms the hotel's windows into blinking eyes of red and gold. My lengthened shadow merges with the opaque night. Entering my room, I startle the famous author, who gapes up at me from his writing desk with wide eyes that seem vacant, or elsewhere. An indian woman, sitting on the bed, is embroidering with colored threads on one of my own white shirts. Without looking up, she says in a soft, kind voice, "Accept this gift as your destiny." Suddenly aware of footsteps in the room above, a bell clanging from the chapel on the hill, a fly bumping on the window pane, odor of coffee, fried eggs and tortillas from the kitchen below, the dust, suspended and vibrating in the liquid light of dawn ... I return to my writing.

CHEZ ROGET

I'M SEARCHING THROUGH THE ROOMS of a Gothic mansion trying to locate a thesaurus. In one gaudy bedroom with satiny fleur-de-lis wallpaper I find Adolf Hitler on a big canopy bed with a sexy blonde, perhaps a prostitute. Both of them wear nothing but black lace garter belts, nylons, and skimpy black brassieres.

Hitler removes a thesaurus from under a pillow and shoves it at me demanding I read him something amusing. He then begins acting like a baby, grimacing in a peculiar way, while bouncing on the bed on his hands and knees. The lady spanks his bare bottom trying to excite him further as well as participate in his exuberant playfulness. But he angrily pushes her away, bouncing higher on the bed, all the time making silly faces at me and fluttering his lips. His tiny moustache looks like a spastic caterpillar.

I mumble to myself, "O good, the dream people," back out of the room and fumble into another. There I find members of the Senoi tribe who live in an equally ornate yet furnitureless boudoir. There's a blue fire burning in the middle of the floor. A young man mimes he wants my sweatshirt with a woven snake mandala on it. So I trade it for a tiny, perfectly preserved bird skeleton tied to a string, which I hang around my neck to *oohs* and *ahhs* from his companions. I sit on the floor next to a bearded child, who, it turns out, is a world-famous anthropologist. My quest for a thesaurus is forgotten as I am engrossed in an intriguing conversation about "transitionary images in cyberspace similar to projections to and from the Egyptian Tuat, Tibetan bardos, and Mayan Xibalba …." Something like that. I comment, "Yes, we are in The Place of Awe." The young man in my sweatshirt is standing inside the blue fire, holding his hands over his ears.

Eventually the room fades dark like a movie has ended, so I wander out and return to the first bedroom to retrieve that thesaurus from Hitler. On entering I find him alone on the bed eating chocolate cake and ice cream with a plastic serving spoon. He tells me to help myself. So I do. And it tastes *great! delicious! excellent! outstanding! superb! scrumptious!*

*H*UNGRY AND THIRSTY AFTER
a long bike-ride downtown, I go to a supermarket, where I encounter
two muscular body-builders, a man and a woman. We are admiring
various cuts of meat in a rotating display case. They open the case and
gather up steaks in their smooth bulging arms as fast as they can. This
muscular duo is blonde and, they tell me, Swedish. He says in an excited
voice, "How great is America! All this meat!" They're both wearing
leopard-skin bikini briefs on their tanned, oiled bodies. I admire her
physique and whisper into her hair, "You are absolutely amazing." He
nudges me with an elbow and says, "You steal my woman, yah?" I reply,
"Yah!" We laugh. I notice he has smeared blood on me from the steaks
clutched in his arms. She croons, "O, I know what you need ..." and
proceeds to give me a massage with her strong hands. I am in ecstasy.

We leave the market together, the woman continuing to rub my back.
Outside, much is happening in the parking lot. Two fat women in black
silk outfits are fighting kung-fu style in a makeshift arena amongst the
cars. A number of people are doing strangely erotic contortions that
seem physically impossible. I exclaim, "Wow, this is just like a dream!"
Crossing the circus-like lot we meet a well-dressed little man with a
goatee and a turban. He appears to be in a trance while drawing
symbols on a cheerleader's pennant. When he "comes to" he explains,
"This is how I access the Mystical Library." I inquire, "Can you get *Out
of The Body Experience*?" He says, "No, but I can levitate." Then chuckles
at his joke. He tells us Sacred Hard Copy can be acquired by astral mail
order from Tibet. "You contact them and get Hot Wired!" he says,

laughing again. Then he simply floats away, like an inflated doll. I examine the pennant he's left behind—it says *Bardo Dodgers*.

The body-builders relax with me, sharing chocolate bars, on a low stone wall in the shade of a palm tree. Finding a book in the dirt there, its title *La Tête Léger*, I ask the muscle man if he knows French. He says, "Oui. It means the way a woman does her hair, like a bun." His girlfriend titters, but I don't get it. Realizing I'll never score with my incredibly well-built masseuse, I bid them "adieu." Anyway, I must rendezvous with Miles Davis on a streetcorner at noon.

Pedalling off, I arrive in time to catch Miles hanging out with a tall, svelte African lady in pink hot pants. She has decorative scars on her face, and cowrie shells and feathers worked into her finely braided hair. Her almond-shaped brown eyes are piercingly "other-worldly." I consider trying to woo this magnificent woman, but am intimidated by Miles. He reads my mind, and says in his raspy voice, "Don't forget, joker, the allure of women is not in the *flash*, but in the *sustained complexity*." Then gives me his scarred-lip grin that isn't a grin. Thick blue smoke curls around our legs. Our tryst apparently over, Miles wheezes, "What it is!" slaps my hand, then he and the lady slide into his red Ferrari and purr away down the avenue.

I climb onto my bicycle and begin the long ride home. Musing on what's occurred during the trip, I compose my face into a mask of cool nonchalance. Back near the supermarket, the two striking Swedes are hitch-hiking beside the road. She's holding up a sign that reads: *We Love's Body*. Hurtling past, I wave and shout, "Bon chance!" Notice he's still carrying a stack of steaks in his tanned, muscular, bloody arms.

THE ORDINARY WORLD

"This is not hell, it is a street. This is not death, it is a fruit stand."
—FEDERICO GARCÍA LORCA.

I ARRIVE IN HADES, BUT IT'S not a land of terrifying fire and molten rock as expected, instead this looks like the ordinary world—blue sky, green grass, streets lined with office buildings, trees, houses, stores. The ordinary world, of ordinary things, I muse, shaking my head in wonder.

Walking a crowded downtown street at noon hour, I say out loud, "These people are dream figures, *and* they are dead!" Those persons nearby stop to stare at me in a manner like the disciplining glare a parent gives a child. Embarrassed by my outburst, I make a joke about *seeing without eyes*, but no one laughs, so I hurry along.

Crossing onto the next block I encounter a "bag lady" wearing four or five layers of clothing and pushing a shopping cart filled with crushed beer cans, bottles, and newspapers. She comes directly up to me, grabs the front of my shirt with a filthy mittened hand, and snarls, "Will anyone please *excuse me*, if for a thoughtless moment the whole fucking world bursts into flame?" Startled by her fury, I do not know what or how to respond. Thankfully she lets go and scuttles off through the crowd like a rattling garbage scow amongst sleek sailing ships.

Suddenly there's a loud *pop!* and I can't hear a thing! I'm deaf. The busy street is hushed, not a sound, despite the cars, trucks, buses, active throngs. Freaked, looking wildly about, I notice a tall building sway as if made of rubber, a fire hydrant chase a dog, a lamp post with open mouth and arms as if singing an aria, a dancing tree holding cartoon birds in its branching hands. I marvel again, if this is truly Hades, it sure isn't what I imagined it to be.

There's another *pop!* like a burst balloon, and I can hear again, only everything's painfully loud. Running to catch up with the cranky homeless woman, I grip her elbow to stop her, then whisper in a conspiratorial way, "You know, mam, When It All Comes Down, I'll be ready. I've practiced moving through these transparent avenues of noise and confusion. I know what it's like to shake hands with the dead." She glowers, gives a knowing wink, then punches me in the mouth.

CANDYMAN

*F*LEEING A SUCCESSION OF misadventures in Europe, I take the ferryboat across the Straits to Morocco. My traveling companion since Málaga has been a haunted, emaciated junkie resembling a concentration camp survivor. I chidingly ask what prison he was in. He answers, "Planet Earth." I must lose this guy, paranoia is *exactly* what I don't need.

We're out on the open deck with the cars. Across the way I recognize a buddy of mine from the Army I haven't seen in over four years!—a tall black man who calls himself the Candyman. I rush over and we have a cheery reunion, amazed by this coincidence. When he laughs I see that gold front tooth sparkle, the one with a star-shaped diamond set in it I used to tease him about in Nam. I'd say, "Best not sleep with your mouth open, sucker. Charlie can buy a lot of guns with that tooth."

Candyman introduces his two silent henchmen. I immediately forget their names, as they're unpronounceable. I can't guess their nationalities. The trio is crossing to Tangier to smuggle a load of primo hashish in secret compartments in their car, drive it to their windmill hide-out near Amsterdam. I do a double-take on his partners, thinking I see a superimposed image of a lizard on each face, as if that's what they really are, only pretending to be human. I shiver with dread, wondering if I've bailed from one doomed adventure to another. But Candy is such a funny fast-talking rogue I'm soon caught up in the excitement of his enterprise.

Arriving in Tangier we go directly to a hotel just off the Socco Chico called *Le Paradis*. The pillared, sunken lobby, as well as our room, has tiles of intricate, exquisite design covering walls and floors. These tiles, as I stare at them, seem "cinematic," each one an abstract, hallucinated movie. Our room is less than paradise however, with no beds, merely crude mattresses on the floor, no furniture, and a bathroom simply a hole in the floor, serving as toilet and drain for a shower that emits what looks like a recirculation of what went into the hole. I think we're mad to stay here, but Candy winks, and insists it's a "perfect" location.

That night, after feasting on "lion-meat" couscous prepared with scorching spices at a café run by a Belgian imp who'd retired from the drug trade, we are guided by a blind arab to the hashish factory—on the outside a nondescript building, but on the inside a cavernous warehouse only entered on hands and knees through a tiny swinging door. I scare myself imagining maybe the door doesn't swing the other way.

The pungent narcotic odor of tons of hashish sucks the air from my lungs making me woozy. Various grades, in differently colored paper-wrapped bricks, are stacked high everywhere. Mountains of sweet shit. There's an ancient crusted table in the middle where old men are working machines that resemble waffle irons recovered from a Pharaoh's tomb, compressing the hash and imprinting each brick with seals of grade and origin. Peering through the gloom and smoke I'm shocked to see the old men are not men at all but snout-faced creatures, like giant rats, with blue-tinged knobby skin. When I shakenly point this out to Candyman, he hisses, "Shh! Don't say a word. Otherwise we'll never leave this place." I'm trembling and want to run, but am paralyzed, head spinning, pulse thudding in my ears.

Not soon enough the transaction is completed, Candy handing over a briefcase to a fat naked white man smoking a giant hookah on a platform overlooking the factory floor. We hurriedly crawl out of there into fresh night air, and I'm relieved I've escaped a land of the dead, or the nearly so. Saying this to Candy amuses him greatly. He slaps me on the back and laughs, saying, "Hey, man! Just like those *dinky-dau* days in Nam!" as we sprint through a maze of alleys up to the *Dancing Boy Café*, where we take a table on a balcony overlooking the lights of the harbor. As we'd entered I'm sure a vulture was standing on a table of a side room.

Glancing at the robed figures around us, I'm stricken with another wave of nausea—I can't see any faces, or bodies, the robes are empty, worn by ghosts! Just then, musicians begin playing a wild ecstatic tune and a young boy dressed like a girl in trailing silks and veils appears, dancing, jingling a tambourine. Swirling to a stop beside me the veil drops and I see with horror his painted face is stitched together, with black button eyes and a mouth of red thread, like a ragdoll. This jerky, bewitched creature then lays his head on my lap while wiggling his behind, to yelps of laughter from the "phantom" crowd. I rise up, knocking over my chair, but Candy waves his hand indicating I should sit back down and relax. Putting an arm around my shoulder he says with a chuckle, "Dig the *spirit*, brother."

After all that's happened, and too many bowls of kif, I'm ready to bid Candyman good-bye and take off on my own. But I don't know how, I feel ensnared by his powerful charisma, especially after he shows me his switchblade and the pistol he keeps in a coat pocket. As if sensing my mood, he mutters under his breath, "We're in this together. Right, amigo? To the *righteous* end. Remember that time in Bien Hoa we surprised those VC copping short-times at the *Bam Bam Club*?" I can only reply, "Uh, sure, man, of course. How forget? To the end. Yes, a *righteous* end."

I don't know how, but we make it back to our hotel room, after meandering through labyrinthine streets of fearful creeping darkness, where every shadow contained a threat of death to my crackled mind. Flopping onto my mattress, I pretend to fall asleep. Later, when the others are snoring, I get up, grab my backpack and slip downstairs into the night, illuminated now by a full moon. I spend the remaining spooky hours until dawn wandering a realm inhabited by leering misshapen figures, whether human, animal or from outer space I couldn't say. I simply keep moving until the sun finally rises and I stumble bleary-eyed into another hotel, hopefully far from where I began, but no way I'm sure of that.

Unfortunately, as it is Ramadan and the city is filled with the faithful come to observe this holy month, the concierge informs me I'll have to share a room. I think, well what else can I do? I need to rest. I need sleep. I need to hide. So I say, "Bien, c'est parfait. I'll take it." I go up, open the door—I'm stunned—there's the Candyman, sitting on the edge of a bed, cleaning a long hooked thumbnail with his switchblade. When he raises his head and smiles, I am blinded by a brilliant flash of gold, a diamond star at its center.

ON THE BORDER

*F*ROM ANOTHER ROOM, A TINNY phonograph plays the same mournful *canción* over and over, again and again. All doors are open in the oppressive heat—near midnight and 90°. Cheap wine will not quench the thirsty need to be gone. It's unbelievable how much one can sweat without even moving. The hotel clerk, a stooped Chinese man, shuffles down in his shorts to bring him the fan from his own room. He doesn't understand why he does this. Obligation? Pity? The clanging fan barely stirs the dead air. June bugs and spiders are everywhere, on and in everything.

Out in the hallway, a brown-skinned woman of indeterminate age, in only bra and half-slip, slides back and forth against the walls as if needing support. After passing a few times, she slumps against the doorjamb and stares in with battered eyes begging what she knows he nor anyone else can provide. Her expression is of total defeat, caught in a play with a script long since discarded—no lines, no action, no resolution. The duration of their exchanged dull stares is painful. With a weak moan, she slinks away. He's bedeviled in this town, where drunkenness and violence seem the norm. His nerves are burnt, fizzled out.

Leaning on his duffel he scrawls a postcard: *Here I am again, in the sad heart of America, little money, no ride, but no regrets. Mañana I hit the Coast, if lucky. Hasta luego? Hang loose.* He lays back to watch a tarantula do push-ups on the dresser. Switching off the lamp to minimize bugs, red neon *JESU AVES* splashes onto the opposite wall, filling the room with the clear light of a night that doesn't end.

He dreams he's doing a funny shuffle-dance in a room with a jukebox and some wooden chairs. He's thinner, younger, and barefoot, wearing only Army fatigue pants. His torso gleams with sweat. A window opens onto pristine darkness. An Hispanic man and woman in their underwear, arms around each other, lean against a wall watching him through heavy-lidded eyes. He discovers he can alter the tempo of the music by dancing "freer." An old woman in black dress and shawl enters, hands him a short length of rope, shouts something in Spanish, like a warning, but he doesn't understand. After she leaves, he sees the rope's a rattlesnake. Then he's in an abandoned boxcar preaching an "uncertain sermon" to men from his unit in Nam. Although their eyes are open, they're not listening—they're all dead.

He's awakened roughly. The Chinaman wants his fan back.

SCI-FI HOTEL

*M*Y GIRLFRIEND AND I GO TO a movie house that's also a hotel. After purchasing tickets we are given the key to Room 222. A pretty young woman in a sequined, tasseled bikini and bathing cap is rushing around trying to get the theater ready to open. She breathlessly explains it is the American premiere of a Japanese science-fiction film, and everyone is tremendously excited. The manager is a cantankerous old character who scoots around in a motorized wheelchair barking, "More sushi! More popcorn shrimp!" He reminds me of Howard Hughes.

We go up to our room for a "quickie" before the film starts, but first I have a desperate need to pee, so limp along the hallway in search of a toilet. I'm lightheaded, like I could pass out. Blundering into room after room looking for a toilet, I repeat, "Pardon me" in, I fear, a much-too-loud voice. Actually, I can only see vague shapes through my vertigo, and feel foolish and disoriented.

Luckily I find our room and sprint to the back where I hope to locate a bathroom. I do, but there are chunks of plaster and other debris on the floor and the toilet is overflowing with a brinish tidepool effluence. I stagger along into another room where I discover a little boy in a crib made of driftwood. He's apparently been abandoned here. He's cute, but has fine black lines or cracks on his face giving him an "antique" appearance; also his head is abnormally large for his body, which emits an odor of rotten fish. There are note papers, like school work, laid on top of him, along with a curling photograph of the child held by a woman I presume to be his mother, but whose face is hidden behind a

Japanese-style fan. I notice she is wearing flippers. One scrap, in a crayon scrawl, says the boy is a problem in school, and his name is "Urchin."

Carrying the silent, fish-eyed child, I return to the front room, only to find my girlfriend has stacked dozens of mattresses on top of each other to the ceiling. Taken aback, I ask her, "How can we possibly make love on such a huge, awkward pile!" Then I hand her the child, which she hugs, coos, and weeps over. My dizziness is unabated. And I still need to "go."

After a hurried discussion, we carry the boy downstairs to the lobby and set him on the candy counter, explaining to an insane-looking usher with "Einstein" hair that we found this baby in our room. But he ignores us, as does everyone else, as they're frantically trying to figure out how to get the film going—it requires some technical adjustment. I tell the lady in the sparkling bikini I know how to fix it, as soon as I relieve myself. She stares at me with a stupefied, despondent look, then chirps, "OK, sure, why not?" I suspect the child is hers, as they have the same bulging fish-eyes, but she's too distracted to be interrogated, and I must get this movie started.

After a fast trip to the men's room, ankle-deep in brackish salt water and kelp, which, in my desperate condition, doesn't bother me, I do manage to get the film rolling by throwing a secret switch at the base of the projector. I can't explain how I know it's there, but no one asks, everyone's so happy it's running. We all troop inside the dark theater and take our seats …

Radioactive leaks from a nuclear power plant have caused a lobster to mutate into a 100-foot-long monster that click-clacks around the countryside scissoring Army tanks and soldiers in two with razor-sharp claws, eventually lumbering into downtown Tokyo, where it knocks over buildings and smashes cars with its hideous tail, terrorizing the inhabitants, who run screaming through the destroyed chaotic streets, holding their faces, making wildly exaggerated gestures of cinema terror. Then a nerdy rogue scientist, mocked earlier for his theory that marine crustaceans are simply bored down there and constantly seek ways "up the evolutionary ladder," manages to lure the creature into a volcano filled with melted butter by having sexy girls in lobster outfits do a can-can on a big-screen video placed on a raft in the middle of the crater. *The End*, to much applause.

When the lights come on, we're up to our frontal lobes in seaweed, and I have to go.

MELUSINA

*M*Y HANDS REACH THROUGH A wall of bread dough to massage the wonderful breasts of a young woman wearing a robe of peacock feathers. As she peels off her gown I hear a graceful rustling of wings sounding like "Liszt." She pulls me through the wall, giggling all the while, saying, "That tickles." Her name is Melusina. Or Melisma. But maybe Stella or Belladonna, I'm not exactly sure.

She and I settle into an old-fashioned bathtub with lion paws and cobra faucet. We make complicated, exciting love following detailed instructions she reads in a bubbly voice off the label of a bottle of love potion. At our most intertwined climax I realize she is as much fish as woman, more serpent than fish, yet more delicate than a butterfly, ravishing as a summer storm.

After dressing each other in clothes made of a clinging sticky substance, I wander off to my study. When I return to the darkened hallway to look for her again, I slide open a door onto a brightly-lit surgical room. She is splayed out on a white sheet on an operating table! With horror I see she's been divided up into pieces, not bloody and gory, but in clean specific, anatomical parts—legs, arms, head, torso, like a store manikin taken apart. A skull-faced doctor with swollen ugly eyes leans over her with a laser-beam scalpel in his skeletal hand. His incisions follow blue dotted lines he's tattooed on her, or she always had?

I try my best to rescue my love, using a knife, a baseball bat, then a pistol, but fail miserably each time. Nothing works to stop this monster, The Doctor, who looms over me in a black butcher's smock, (black with its history of blood, I think) and with an evil grin sneers, "You cannot kill *me*, you fool. I am the Lord of Death!" I flee from this terrible gut-wrenching scene, knowing I will never forget, and possibly never understand.

I run off into a rat-maze, helter-skelter, eventually finding an open door into utter darkness, through which I hurl myself in a great flight that carries me out past Pluto, into a cold starry night of emptiness and loss, where, I suspect, I linger much too long. Finally returning to earth from this "purgatorial" region of outer space, wrapped in a cocoon of self-pity and hurled like a spear by an unknown force, I land in the middle of a downtown intersection, only to be grabbed by police convinced I am an escaped convict. "This is *not* fantasy," I calmly explain, "This is Natural Magic and True Religion." But they do not believe, and torture me with "The Spider" in a basement containing a dozen small mounds of salt set in a pentacle around me. On top of each pile is a burning black candle. My body has been painted red, and I hang upside down, wrists and ankles bound with a silver rope.

With a conscious effort to "straighten up," I escape by coolly walking out the front door humming a tune perfectly synchronized to the throbbing heart of the city. I then smuggle myself onto a sailing ship bound for my home country. Once we're underway, I leave my hiding place and sneak into the wheelhouse, where I am astonished to see the same fearsome Doctor. I watch transfixed as he meticulously transplants the brain of a Romantic poet into a small dog that's also had the wings of a large bird grafted to its spine. After the operation, the dog does a wild flight around the room, bumping into windows and walls, then drops into the spidery arms of the Doctor, whose hideous laughter sounds like ripping sails in a storm.

"Dreams perpetuate their impetuous race," I hear him cackle, as I warily back away towards the lifeboat, slip beneath its tarp cover. There I find the beautiful Melusina! who claps a hand over my mouth, giggles, then whispers, "Dreams bring the background forward. And life is renewed."

I wake up next day in the lifeboat, alone, floating along the Milky Way, in a rush-hour stream of traffic.

THE NEW LOOK

*M*ANEUVERING A LARGE DELIVERY truck through jammed streets of a big city, I'm lost most of the time. At last, I reach my destination, driving into a block-long warehouse, also a grocery store. The clerk is a robust old hag who clambers up into the cab to collect money from me and inspect the food I'm delivering. I'm not sure how much I owe her, and wonder if I'm supposed to pay at all. Shouldn't it be the other way around? I withdraw a bill from my wallet, and holding it out, I see it's a two-dollar bill with Billie Holiday's picture on it! I say to the hag, "Sorry ... Lady Day." And stuff the bill into my shirt pocket.

I stash the rest of my money and personal belongings in an iron box, not trusting the wily old woman nor her shadowy helpers not to steal my stuff, or do me harm. Looking around for a place to hide the box, I notice long banquet tables laden with all kinds of goodies and food, like it's Thanksgiving, but there are no chairs, nor any guests. There are ladders everywhere rising out of sight into the darkness above; and colorful paintings by children taped on the walls. This must be a school as well.

Scanning the upper reaches of this expansive building, I'm surprised to see my father, sitting casually in an ornate, curtained balcony like he's enjoying a concert or a movie. I climb up through a spiraling tubular ladder to reach his perch. Elated to see him, I cry out, "What are you doing here!?"

Dad patiently explains he's decided to change his "look." He has long, slicked-back hair (unlike his usual crewcut) and a pencil-line moustache. And he's wearing a broad-shouldered, silk zoot suit of wide pinstripes, a carnation in a lapel, looking like a silent film star. He says in a proud, serious voice he now wants to be known as "Carmen Alejandro." And he's become a wandering troubadour, a singer of ballads and love songs!

I think, well, he's all right, he's OK, and drive away feeling pretty good about this "new look" of his.

GHOST BEAR

A MAN AND WOMAN ARE TAKING a long hot drive out into the desert to visit a Native American friend he'd known in the war, Ghost Bear. Using a worn crude map he's carried in his wallet since Ghost Bear had given it to him years before, they arrive at an isolated hogan, miles off the main highway. Greeting an old man sitting in the shade of a giant saguaro, they learn he's his friend's grandfather. Sorrowfully, he tells them Ghost Bear had gone out into the desert one day about a year ago and hasn't been seen since. The grandfather believes he's dead. He thinks so because when his grandson had walked away, he'd seen a "sunset cloud" follow him. The old man tells them, "That means *death*."

Saddened, the man walks a few paces away, kneels in the sand, scoops up a handful, pours it on his head, rubs it in his face, throws some in the air, then cries with deep sobs. The grandfather goes over, helps him up, embraces him, saying, "You're the one to find him. Yes, maybe you can. With my help." The man chokes, "But if he's dead, what good will it do to find his bones?" "Ah," says the old man, "if you find him, you will discover *more* than just bones. There'll be a *vision*. You can be sure." The man looks into the ancient face of the other, imagines he sees a coyote inside the dark eyes of that deeply-lined face. Shaking his head, he stammers, "What should I do?"

The old man hands him a leather pouch and says, "Tonight, before sunset, you must eat the pollen in this bag and walk into the desert the way I indicate. If you keep your eyes open, and the pollen will aid you, and do not fear whatever you see or hear, you will locate Ghost Bear.

Don't worry about your lady friend, she'll be fine." The man looks at her with that wondering expression, "What do you think?" She responds, "I know we came all the way out here for *something*. You might as well find out what it is. I'll be all right. Just take care."

A few hours later the man has eaten the bag of "pollen" and is striding in the direction of a large rock starkly outlined by the setting sun. The pollen seems to be an hallucinogen. He feels euphoric and energized, slightly dizzy and disoriented. Nevertheless, he stays true to the rock, and ignores the rustling, writhing, hissing, and crackling sounds he hears on each side of his passage. It is fairly easy going, the ground is flat, with only low mesquite to hinder a perfectly straight course.

Although it is a moonless night, he's able to see just as well as if it were daylight. Thanking the old man for the pollen, which seems to have given him this power, he trudges on, thinking of Ghost Bear, and the good and terrible times they'd shared in the war. He remembers with a smile the time Ghost Bear had gotten drunk, grabbed the hated First Sergeant, thrown him over his shoulder like a bag of rice, and dropped him down the shithole. A court martial was averted when the Major himself stood up for Ghost Bear, not wanting to lose one of his best soldiers. Nevertheless, Ghost Bear was on permanent shit-burning detail.

After an hour of steady walking, the man comes to the rock, which he discovers is in fact a twenty-foot statue carved from a single stone. Walking around, running his hands over it, he determines it is a totem with animals stacked atop each other—bear, coyote, eagle, rattlesnake, jackrabbit. He notices an inverted V-shaped split in the back of the totem and peers in. As he does so a beam of light from directly above illuminates the statue and a wide circle around it. Staggering backwards onto his behind, he is terrified as a monstrous rattlesnake emerges from the hole, rears up and flicks its forked tongue. Inside his head he hears, "Stay calm. Sit still. Relax your vision. Fear not."

While struggling to do just that, the man finds himself face to face with his friend, and blurts out, "Ghost Bear!" But Ghost Bear simply puts his finger to his lips and points straight up at the source of light engulfing the area. Looking up, the man is puzzled to see a patch of blue in the night sky. And around the rim of turquoise—a circle of faces peering down. These faces seem so familiar … then he realizes they're all *himself* at different periods of his life—age six, nine, twelve, sixteen, nineteen, twenty-one, each face reflecting a unique "tragic knowledge" particular to each era—what he truly *was* at various crucial times.

Understanding, but not quite, he asks Ghost Bear, "Are they really so different? Isn't there a way to know all these changes as *one*?" Ghost Bear nods in the affirmative and points again, this time at an amber full moon, fat and bright above the jagged mountains. Staring into it with tears down his face, the man slowly rises, and returns, seeing there's no other way to go—holding his *vision* like an owl its prey, or a bear, the scent of honey.

MYSTIC

"Forever arriving, you will go everywhere." —RIMBAUD.

$\mathcal{F}$EARFULLY, I WALK OUT INTO the expansive night alone, heading towards the heart of a forest. I do this in order to locate the grave of Arthur Rimbaud. Finding a cemetery I climb an iron gate and drop down into tall wet grass filled with spider webs that cling to my legs. Reading headstones in the dark with my fingers, I determine one is a radio, with a single dial that switches power on and adjusts volume. The crackling adolescent voice of Rimbaud comes on. He indicates his location is not far, and describes the way, "There's a skull-lined path leads from the cemetery to where I am. I'll keep broadcasting until you arrive."

After thrashing around in a thorny patch, I find and follow the macabre walkway for torturous miles, finally through a strand of moonlit desert, up to a dark, abandoned farmhouse. Pulling on a broken screen door, I enter a pitch-black room. A red light shines in my face, causing me to jump with a gasp. The light is set in the forehead of a hideous zombie, who growls, "Welcome to the village of the living dead."

Retreating outside, I stumble over a dog and fall. The dog is large, fluffy, powder blue, and glows as if radioactive or made purely of electric blue light. Its hot fetid breath burns my face. A good situation to use alchemical magic, I muse, as the dog licks my neck tickling me, until I realize in horror that like a vampire the dog is draining my life! I pass out before I'm able to try any magic.

I come to in a cemetery, covered with fresh dirt. It smells acrid as nervous sweat. There's damp soil in my eyes, ears, and mouth. Sitting up gagging, I spit, clear my throat, and launch into the *Voyant* section of the epic poem I've been working on these many years. I plan to finish the opus, dedicated to A.R., as soon as we arrive across this perfumed abyss.

FLIGHT

OUTSIDE THE ENTRANCE TO a carnival, I'm waiting with a lovely young woman who wears an extravagant lacy, white dress, like a wedding dress. I inquire if that's what it is. She giggles, and exclaims, "Oh, don't be such an idiot!" then turns sharply away. As she whirls, the scene shifts, like a positive photograph to a solarized version. I find myself alone in a field of blue grass under an orange sky.

Deciding to vanish I sit on a wooden chair beside me, which takes off! But as it ascends it wobbles, and I find it difficult to hang on, as the chair has no arms or place for feet. I soon gain altitude, but the chair has no steering wheel either, and as it totters I'm sure I'll topple out. Then I discover it operates with an inflated bag held under the arm like bagpipes—squeezing on the bag causes the chair to accelerate.

I swoop through a lush tropical canyon, then soar out over a town just above telephone poles and power lines. At first I am at a loss as to how to steer the chair, but eventually manage by directing it with my *attention*—it goes in the direction willed. I fly swiftly and soundlessly. Not able to get over looming buildings and tall trees, I deftly swerve around them. I feel self-conscious in this flying chair; this isn't something I should be doing in daylight.

I zoom over a neighborhood of shanties and tenements. Directly below there's a gang of tough-looking guys playing ball. The chair sinks downwards, but I pump on the bag and rise sharply over a tall apartment building, where everything on the roof is in super-sharp focus: the white gravel, cigarette butts, wires, ventilation ducts, broken bottles, a speckled cat. I float up over the building then slowly descend, setting down perfectly in a parking space next to a sidewalk, like a rocket ship docking in outer space.

I've landed in front of an arcade of small shops beneath an awning, like a Mexican mercado, its stalls filled with crafts, foodstuff, clothing. A robust, but not fat, middle-aged woman with another woman, perhaps her sister, are ahead of me as I walk into the arcade. This first woman is extremely attractive, with large breasts, good posture, shiny black hair, strong legs on high heels, and in a tight red dress that accentuates her sexy walk. She has full lips and dark, glowing eyes.

Turning to wait for her sister, this woman gives me the eye and smiles flirtatiously. We're inside an open stall, and I'm more-or-less stuck in front of her as there isn't space to walk around. Then someone screams, "A snake!" I look over to see it wriggling on a shelf, perhaps an altar, containing candles, flowers, photos in tarnished frames, bundles of herbs, talismans, fetishes of dried animals and birds tied up with colored string. The writhing snake is knocking things onto the floor.

Glancing back at the woman, I realize she's not as beautiful as I'd thought—her lipstick's on crooked, she has on too much cakey make-up, her hair's dirty, the dress is frayed and split at a seam, and her perfume is nauseating. To my amazement, this strange woman reaches over and grabs the snake in one swift motion, holding it out in her hand with a look of triumph and power. Then she wheels toward me.

The snake, golden yellow with a diamond pattern, is contorting and hissing in her grip. I hear rattles but don't see any. Someone sprays what looks like blue paint on the snake's head, apparently to stun it, but this doesn't stop it from wildly striking at the air. Instead of removing the serpent as expected, the woman shoves it at me! The agitated snake bites twice in quick succession, once inside my right bicep, leaving a "tattoo" from the blue sprayed on it, and secondly at the ribs, just below my thudding heart.

Although there's no pain, I know I've been hit, gawking at the paint-smeared impression of the snake's head on my arm, with distinct fang marks. The woman is now braying, showing big ugly teeth smeared with lipstick, as she taunts me, amused by my predicament, my inability to flee, my confusion and fear. She does an obscene bump'n'grind, swaying broad hips, rubbing her sex against my leg like an animal in heat. I am faint, white stars dance in my eyes, my brain gone numb.

Suddenly this mad lady and I are together in a bare, white-washed adobe room. Although it has no obvious doors or windows, I don't feel trapped, instead, I feel "light" and released. The woman's now wearing a frilly white, old fashioned dress with many petticoats, and is much changed, seeming innocent and nice, even virginal. Smiling sweetly, she takes my hand and speaks softly close to my face, in a reassuring, musical voice, "Listen, my love, when you enter the festival, greet every person you meet like they're someone *special*. Show them you *care*. Make sure they understand you are dead *too*."

CALYPSO

A MAN HAS CRYSTALS STRAPPED to his body to protect him from the liquescent personality of an enchanting lady. Thus, he is able to admire her shifting beauty up close without getting entangled in her various mad schemes. Or so he imagines. He boasts, "I have numerous personalities, one for each of you." She nods, regarding him with her usual, fathomless, sly humor.

They're in a café arguing each other senseless over the "body/mind question." He says, "Each night the hunter stalks its prey." She replies, "Only if the hunter is himself not prey." These games progress until a late hour, when he's alone and decides it's time to go home. But he's stopped short, finding all the walls of the café identical and smooth, without windows or doors. He pushes on one wall, but it's a false wall and swings around returning him to where he started. He pushes one after another, yet he's always in the same room over and over again. This goes on for some time. Then, shoving with all his strength, he tumbles into darkness. And screams.

When he opens his eyes, he's inside a cave. Not an ordinary dank cave—this one's scented with perfumes and incense and appears to be inhabited. As his vision adjusts, he sees plush carpets, couches strewn with luxurious pillows, oil lamps burning in golden niches. Investigating an assortment of glass figurines on a table of porphyry, he's suddenly enclosed in the arms of a sweet nymph.

This spirited lady covers his face with ardent kisses like a long-lost lover. As his mind whirls with passion, confusion, and relief, she explains this is her home and he may stay as long as he desires. She also informs him with an eager expression she can "charge his crystals." Hearing this he becomes reflective. Then they're on a couch that, although soft, looks carved from a great ruby. While making love, she brings her feet up and around, placing them behind her head like a sideshow contortionist. In a husky voice she says, "I wonder who is the hunter and who the prey." He gulps.

She then makes a "sandwich" of the two of them between her enchanting self and his egoistic self—"Like playing an octopus accordion," she says with musical laughter and glee. At this point, he can only mentally shrug, enjoy this beatific interlude, his crystals glowing.

BEATNIK PLAY

I'M IN THE ARMY, STATIONED
in the States, when I encounter a high school pal who thinks I'm a
General and salutes me. I explain, "These aren't stars on my shoulder,
they're *power flakes*." We laugh. He says he's enlisted because his wife
won an Oscar and ran off with an Italian actor, who isn't even Italian—
he's an Apache! We laugh again, but I don't know why, as he's in
obvious distress.

We march over to the mess hall where they serve us nothing but
desserts—cakes, pies, muffins, cookies, fudge, candy, ice cream. It's like
a kids' party. I ask the cook where's the usual slop, but he simply glowers
while pouring chocolate syrup over a mound of cupcakes on my tray. I
whisper an aside to my pal, "We'll frag this dope with peanut butter."

There's supposed to be a "Beatnik Play" shown on base tonight. But
it gets canceled after the riot in the mess hall. Back in the barracks, I tell
my bunkmate, Bob Dylan, how disappointed I am. Thinking I'm an
idiot anyway, he ignores me, as he attempts to extricate himself from the
cat's cradle he's made.

I walk around the fort with my rifle loaded at all times, extra bullets
in every pocket. I'm concerned about the *barbarians*, remembering the
unbelievable terror when we ran out of ammo during the Tet Offensive.
I held my breath for three days. I can't forget the opium den where semi-
human protoplasmic slugs oozed poisonous clouds of madness and
despair. But not to partake was to risk another kind of hallucination:
Reality *in extremis*. I sit on my bunk playing solitaire as the roar of
howitzers outside the hootch pulverizes the jungle, the night, my sanity.

My mail keeps getting delivered to random locations. I'll find a package with my name on it practically anywhere. As usual, the one I've found today under a truck has been opened by the censors. I have no idea what they've taken or altered but the dragon-silk pajamas I'd ordered are here. I'm told they render one *incredibly wise*. I'm wearing them right now. I think. No. Excuse me. I'm not.

My pal's been transferred to the Isle of Lethe. Some have all the luck. Hey—no big thing. And to hell with bunkie Dylan, who rummages through my notebooks stealing lines, erasing drawings. He doesn't realize I've taken my lines from his talking dreams. The hell with solitaire, too— I'm now in the Beat Hotel in Paris, busy cutting up this miscreant century.

NIGHT IN THE WORLD

A MAN IS SLEEPING IN A BEDROOM like an igloo staring at a watery book that functions like a telephone. The phone rings. He reluctantly picks it up. It's the Savior on the line, offering a tremendous, once-in-a-lifetime deal on Salvation. The man responds, "No thanks, done that." Hangs up with a splash, teeth chattering.

Meanwhile, the wife of a friend is licking his neck, chewing on his ear, whispering hoarsely, "I'm the crow, the crow, the crow." In a trance he exits La Puerta in order to greet her when she arrives. She's there on the front lawn sitting before a small fire fanning the smoke, cupping hands to drink it. He kneels down beside her to share the silent beauty of their totally different worlds. She utters cryptically, "Everything's already happened." He agrees, totally, but not really.

Outside now, and completely naked, the man encounters his wife in the woods. She smells like dirt, fresh wet dirt. "What a moon," she gushes. He stammers, "O yes, it's night in the world. And we're talking." A troop of tiny golden-haired children cling to her patchwork dress. She carries the scent of mushrooms, and gives him a huge chanterelle. He thanks her, but not in her language. "I don't speak *owl*," he says anyway. She titters, showing pointed yellow teeth, and tells him, "You're not as bare as you think."

Back inside, the house glows with a variety of jewels, everything burnished by their sodden light and heavy perfumes. "Yes, it's night in the world," the man thinks, observing a number of beautiful women lounging around, each in a different hue. One woman runs in place, fleeing from a memory of running in place. Another woman crawls on all fours, sniffing feet and howling. Another wears a sheer silken cocoon and speaks thickly, confiding, "There are women who don't leave traces."

He sees a man in a white bathrobe lying on a couch. Despite the activity this man doesn't stir, but he's not dead. The man knows if the man-in-the-robe wakes up, the women disappear. His friend's wife takes his hand, says, "There you are. Our ship's waiting." Thinking she's a secret agent, he invents an excuse. She says, "All right. But don't forget—There are women who don't leave traces."

He shakes the man in the bathrobe. He doesn't stir, but he's not dead.

LOVER MAN

$\mathcal{A}$ MAN IS HAVING A BEER IN a saloon called the *Casanova*. Around the bar from him he recognizes a famous tenor player—the sad, baggy eyes, stingy-brim hat. He almost shouts over to the jazzman, "Hey, this is Copenhagen." The old tenorman sets his whiskey down in a deliberate manner, looks over forlornly and replies, "No shit." The man nods and smiles, as if sharing a secret, finishes his beer and walks out into blinding sunlight.

The man says out loud with a satisfied air, "Yes indeed, this is Copenhagen all right." Then, realizing it is *night*, and what he'd thought was bright daylight was the neon glare of the nightclub district, he rushes over to Tivoli Gardens, where he's to meet his sweetheart in front of the roller coaster around midnight.

After two a.m. she finally arrives on the back of a giant swan, bearing aloft a bag of Chinese take-out, and another of pastries, a gleam of pleasure on her face. Actually, she *always* has a gleam of total delight on her face. That's the kind of woman she is. As well as vivacious, blonde, statuesque, and clairvoyant, in a haphazard sort of way. She also has a "perfect" mole on her cheek, and a tattoo of a phoenix encircling her navel.

They sit on a wrought-iron bench beneath a tree strung with Christmas lights to enjoy egg rolls and other munchies. They eat in silence awhile, then he asks her to run away with him to Morocco, where they can "make love in peace." Her response is to weep and tell him about a certain Monkeyman who hounds her everywhere. The man says, "I understand." When, of course, he most certainly does not.

By now fog has swept in and Tivoli dissolves in mist. Rising with a sigh the man hikes back to his hotel, a bordello, to participate in an orgy for the benefit of some wealthy voyeurs. Awkward at first, he soon learns to ignore the presence of the nonparticipants and achieves many stunning results, eliciting gasps and hushed hurrahs from the audience. After collecting his split, paid by a ravishing lady with crossed-eyes and an insatiable appetite for ecstasy, the man takes a cab over to *Club Martyrium*, a jazz hall.

Through the hashish haze, he's happy to see the great tenor player on the bandstand in the midst of a miraculous solo that lasts an entire set. After closing time, the man retrieves his backpack and boards a train for the south. Seated in his compartment, he stares out onto the station platform at the dazzling blonde with the stunning smile who is not there to say good-bye. He recalls her last words as they stood beneath a misty streetlight: "To know this is a dream, is the first step." The man sits back, closes his eyes, and hums the improvised break on "Lover Man" he remembers so well from that legendary time.

FROM AN EYE

*E*NTERING AN OFFICE BUILDING, I go into the lavatory to examine my irritated left eye. I lean over the sink, peer into the mirror to focus on what may be causing the problem. Viewing the eye up close, I notice a small protuberance sticking out of the center of the pupil. Grasping it carefully between thumb and little finger I give it a firm tug, withdrawing it from my eye. In doing so I do not wince, nor feel any pain.

Studying this thing, I see it's a silver rod about an inch long, like a thick pin, but with blunt ends. Scrutinizing closer, it doesn't seem to be metallic, maybe wood or bone, rather than plastic or steel. Tiny beads of blood cling to it but there was no bleeding from the eye when I pulled it free, nor is there now.

Standing in an overly bright, glaringly white and chrome bathroom, with humming fluorescent lights and shiny waxed floor, holding this strange "elemental" object, I'm struck by an odd thought: "Which side of the mirror am I on?" And I have the distinct experience of "me" as a Platonic Idea, an abstract form, not "real." Then laughter and voices echo through the room, seemingly far away, and from many directions. Out of this din, I clearly hear, "I from an eye." Although "I" and "eye" sound identical, I know which is which in this phrase. There's another surging wave of laughter and jumbled conversation like a large cocktail party in another room.

Startled by a presence, I suddenly see a naked man in the mirror beside me, who exclaims, "What's this!?" pointing at the "pin" I hold before me. Shifting my attention, I stare dumbly at him, brush past out of the bathroom. In the silent, empty hallway, I'm astonished to see my mother, standing before a window of light at one end of the hall. I shout, "Mom!" and glide over like on roller skates, to place the thing from my eye into her hand. She stares at it a moment; then, looking up, says in a firm voice, "I am *not* your mother. And I have been waiting patiently for your return."

THE PILOT

SOMEBODY'S GOT TO DO IT. So I volunteer to climb the tower to light the pilot connecting mortality to the moon. No problem, I think. Death's "waiting area" is a parking lot adjacent to the golf course. Dad walks by on the sidewalk eating a jelly doughnut. I shout, "Dad!" He mumbles, "Whatcha doin?" I tell him, "I have to light the pilot." He says, "OK, but first, get your ashes hauled, then it'll be smooth going." "All right," I say, "All fuckin' right." However, following further investigations, it's obvious I'm the only one foolish enough for this job. Do I have a choice?

I'm in Paris in a Pig Alley hotel. The "flics" want us out. I order fresh croissants and barricade the door, determined to see this particular trial through. Later, after sneaking down the fire escape with my "day tripper," we're standing in line for an animated version of *The Tibetan Book of The Dead*. From the rooftop I hear, "Dive! Dive!" so we clear out to my favorite dive, *Club La Terminus*. In our booth, I'm pointing out revolutionary graffiti I'd carved on the table in '68, when a Neanderthal-type shoves in demanding I write a letter for him as he's illiterate. I ask, "What do you want me to say?" He grumbles, "This land is covered with ice and we're unconscious because God's stolen our hide." I forgot I must ignite the pilot, so we ditch the doofus and shoot down the ice slide out of there.

Strolling *Boule Mich* I'm wearing two right shoes, both pointed with curved tips. Alfred Jarry bicycles up and says, "What's left!" I respond, "Yes, yes, je ne sais pas." He offers me his broken leg in case I've "gone too far." So I lick his face, apply stamps from Mozambique, grab my girlfriend and take the Metro in the wrong direction. (Remembering Artaud's motto: "When I'm wrong I'm right.")

There's a miniature surveillance satellite hovering over us. So I leave my lady friend in the care of The Man With No Name (Clint Eastwood in a serape), and cut out, slipping into a fancy "house" I know. Groping my way down a red-lit hallway I discover with a pleasant thrill it is filled with naked women lounging on the padded floor. Crawling over this entangled pulchritude I grope an exotic-looking lady with breasts like pamplemousse. I say, "Oops! Excusez-moi." She asks, "Are you the pilot?" I reply, "No, but close." I massage my way through and out the back door to regard a sad moonless sky.

Outside the hotel I fall in love with an ethereal redhead in a trenchcoat and miner's cap mowing an outdoor carpet. She has a jaguar on a golden leash tagging along. I ask if she's been *betrayed* lately. She laughs, saying she was caught in a fire that very morning but managed to "piss" her way out of it. I laugh too while stroking her cat. She tells me its name is "Luna." Which reminds me of my task ... something about a reincarnate forcing itself into the wrong body— mine! Reluctantly I bid her "c'est tout!" and return to the case, hopping a hippie van for ports unknown.

"It's too frighteningly *real*," I report to the Committee back in the States. The Boss says, "Look, fool, just light the damn pilot, then you're free to be as liberated as you wanna be." Recalling what Dad had said, I haul my ashes at "La Mecánica of the Vanishing Point." She has multiple bodies and is hard to keep in focus, yet we do a fierce tango until I'm emptied, so I drift over to a park for a nap. I'm on my back on the soft grass, Panama hat over my eyes ... wake up on the bedroom floor! I think, "This is weird. I'm in two places at once." I stand and tip-toe to the other side of the bed where I locate myself in a canoe on the Seine, and without a paddle. I shout over, "There are demons every-where!" But I roll over and continue drifting merrily along beneath a starry heaven. Which reminds me (again)…so I climb that spiral tower of electrical existence and light the pilot…that the moon may illuminate our tale's dispersion.

RAP

I'M TO RENDEZVOUS WITH SOME Russian cyberpunks to work on a fantastic computer project that will save the world. But I can't locate them and am driving in circles around a warehouse district. Sharply rounding a corner I almost hit a faceless man in a hooded robe leaning against a push cart, posed with arms folded like he's been waiting for me. His cart is filled with an oddly random assortment of trinkets. I get out to ask directions, but he simply shows me an open box of seed packets with a great jazz musician pictured on each cover. I recognize Lester Young, Art Tatum, Eric Dolphy. He tells me, "Take them, they're free! Just always devote the fruit of your work to God. This is the meaning of life." He is Middle Eastern or perhaps Indian. I ask where he's from and his name. He whispers in my ear, "God," then abruptly rolls his rickety cart away.

Still lost in a maze of identical buildings, I decide to leave my car and walk. Soon I encounter a group of Rastafarians with bird cages on their heads, atop their waist-length dreadlocks. Each cage contains a different brightly colored bird. I ask if they know where I might find the place I seek, the one with turrets like the Kremlin. "It can't be missed," I say. They stare uncomprehendingly and sit in a huddle in the street to discuss me, apparently, as they gesture in my direction speaking in a patois I don't understand. One rises and says in a "refined" British voice, "No place in Babylon. You comprehend like anyone, Mistah In-Between-Mon." Then they light up huge spliffs and disappear inside clouds of smoke.

Continuing on, I enter an abandoned factory resembling a Mayan temple, its walls covered with frescoes, glyphs, inscriptions. Finding a blank space I take out a pen and write a long poem about what's happened that day and my dreams from the night before. As I add the last word, a black man in dark glasses with a silver-tipped cane taps by. Recognizing him, I shout, "Rap!" Yes, he knows me, by my honky smell, he says, and we laugh. I blurt, "What are you doing here? I thought you got wasted in Nam?" He looks shocked, says, "But, man, I *was* blown away. Don't you remember? You were right there." "Yes, yes, of course," I mumble, backing off. A loud clanging and banging of cymbals and bells accompanies me out of the dark "temple" into sunlight.

Returning to my car, I find the interior filled with bright blue water! Tropical fish, salamanders, snakes, and frogs swim around inside. There's a note under the windshield wiper. Fearing a ticket, I snatch it off angrily, only to read: "Your poem—Never neglect your rap, my man. Give it up ...."

OPENER OF WAYS

A MAN IS MAKING LOVE TO A gorgeous movie star in the sand beneath a railroad trestle near ocean breakers. They're half-buried in the sand, there's sand in her mouth, sand in her vagina. The man tells her, "It's OK, just shake it out." As she does so she turns herself "inside-out," becomes a lioness that roars and leaps onto the man's back. "Wait!" he screams, "No! This isn't what it is!" He runs staggering down the beach towards the water with the cat clinging to his back, and collapses into the surf. Beneath the waves he finds himself inside a green room and the lioness is once again the beautiful actress. He exclaims, "What was *that* all about!?" She replies with a snarl, "I am the Opener of Ways." The man leaves the green room, walks back up onto the beach, chewing his lip, rubbing his head, spitting salt water.

Next day he writes in his dream journal: "A man is playing maracas for a woman curled on a chair like a house cat. She *is* a cat. The man sets down the maracas and looks up the phrase 'House of Life' in an encyclopedia. He knows he's been there. He gets on his bicycle and pedals through a vivid, spectral wall. On the other side is his teacher, a lovely movie star, whose name he forgets. She grades his dream in red ink, writing 'Sekhmet is not to be trifled with.' He is grateful and gives her a gold chalice filled with sand, saying, 'This is my heart.'" Setting aside his journal, he feels unbalanced and homeless.

Out on the street, pulling a wagon filled with worthless treasures, he encounters two Nubian sisters who lead him to a boat. He loves them both very much, remembering a liminal world they once shared. A ferocious, raving man squats in straw down in the hold of the boat. Asking who the crazy man is, he's told: The Watcher. He then discovers the women are to be sold to an evil being, perhaps the vile creature in the straw? Sleeping between their thin cold bodies, he implores them to look into the future to see if they can avoid slavery. They stare at him mutely with sad dark eyes. Feeling seasick, he puts on his shirt like pants, his pants like a coat, tears them off angrily. "This is crazy!" he shouts in frustration, "Why, these sisters don't even look alike. One's a blonde Hollywood actress, not Egyptian. The other has the yellow eyes of a cat!"

Jumping ship, he returns to the inner city, where he joins a group of tramps on benches in the park. He sits down next to a man wearing a fez and with a drooping white moustache. Startled by the man's penetrating gaze, he quickly turns his attention towards the sun, which feels warm and reviving on his face. The men are telling stories, joking, drinking wine, admiring the flash of legs of passing women. The same beautiful actress strolls by in a tight dress. The fellow in the fez elbows him in the ribs and toggles his bushy eyebrows. But the man pretends he doesn't notice her, nor the trail of sand in her wake, nor the words "House of Life" on the building she enters through an opening in the wall that closes up behind her.

He rises and walks off in the sureness of his great peril.

IN NIGHT TOWN

*H*ANDS DEEP IN COAT POCKETS, I trudge down a rain-damp cobbled lane in a big city. It is early in the century. I sense an eye behind a monstrous lens watching me. I have fallen through a dark place and do not recognize the voice of my thoughts, which is slow and warped like a record at wrong speed. There's a strong sense of bilocation, of being in two places at once, yet I continue walking at this late hour, making little breath clouds in the chill air.

It is far into the night, and quite dark inside a room with wallpaper peeling onto a floor of cracked linoleum, a dripping faucet the only sound. There's a small table and a chair, upon which I sit, wearing a suit and a derby hat. My hands are flat on the table as if in anticipation of someone or something. In fact, I am staring into a lozenge-shaped blob of light that's formed inside my forehead. A grinding is heard in the streets below, and I imagine an atomic bomb released in minute increments.

The light inside my head is a shimmering turquoise triangle that engulfs me. Looking out from this blue haze I am miles above the earth and realize with absolute surety, surprisingly vitalizing, that it is too late to save our planet. I think, "Nothing happens." Then I'm squatting amongst trash in the heart of a city, drinking with cupped hands at a spring gushing from a solid oddly-shaped rock, as if sculpted to look "natural." I rise and bow, knowing I am indeed in two places simultaneously.

The window slides open and a black dog glides into the room. I leap up, grab the dog tightly by its muzzle. My heart is racing. Another dog, a shaggy white animal then enters, followed by a man in a red shirt, with greased-back hair and a pencil-line moustache. He looks like a killer. Hanging onto the dog, I'm visibly shaking. The man says in a calming voice, "All right, all right. It's *not* the end of the world." He climbs back out the window, along with the white dog. With a shudder, I see I'm no longer clutching the black dog but am holding a handful of moonlit water.

The only one out on the streets except for scavenging rats, I grip my coat tighter, pass beneath a flickering gas lamp, turn down another glistening cobbled lane. Catching the moon reflected in a rain puddle, I slow my pace to stare up into the night sky, thinking, "There are two moons—one of rock, the other of light." Hurrying on, I hope that once back in my room, the shape of things will be familiar.

MORNING STAR

A HIGH, WIDE ARCADE HAS multi-colored banners draped ceiling to floor. Each banner, besides having a unique geometric pattern, contains a printed glyph, sign, or numeral inside a white circle at eye level. A man entirely in black enters carrying a star-shaped bladed weapon, as used by ninja warriors. He throws the star through the waving sea of banners, hearing it *thunk!* at the other end. His keen senses tell him he's thrown accurately, through the "4" and the "5." He knows this because of his faith in the "9," figure for Venus, his guardian ally and energy.

After the star hits the wall, a gust parts the banners, and the man has a clear view of the path before him. Approaching stealthily down the hall he finds an open door, and inside a rack set into granite containing letters carved from precious stones—lapis, turquoise, jade. These letters form words in the forgotten language of the Ancients. Some letters are missing, and thus a few words are unreadable. But he has an insight— letters aren't gone, they're simply scrambled. He rearranges them to make whole words. And he remembers what they mean.

At the instant he reads the reformed sentence, he's crossing moors at dawn in a northern country of an earlier century. There's a farm, and brown hills tinged with gold by the rising sun, the farm also streaked with a bronze glow. The air, cool and damp, is thick with the scent of alfalfa, horses, and cows. The scene is hushed, everyone is asleep, including animals. He is alone on a narrow cow path winding around fences, crumbling stone walls, barns, and pens. He notices dark shapes of animals, and steps quietly, not wanting to rouse anyone, especially dogs.

Walking briskly from the farm, he's soon amongst scrubby hills with an occasional twisted cypress clinging to a rocky outcrop. Coming over a rise into a valley, he looks upon a complex of buildings. Without hesitation he strides down and enters a huge wooden barn made of plastic-simulated wood. People in white lab coats have been waiting to show him the "Great Lab," and take him area to area, each containing complex gadgetry, bubbling crucibles, electronic equipment, beeping monitors. They're very proud, and exclaim with broad gestures, pointing at this or that arcane project. He nods his head with a sober expression, acting impressed, although he hasn't a clue as to what the Great Lab is about.

They then usher him into a room opposite the labyrinth of labs, and leave him, departing with satisfied looks. The room is warmed by a brick fireplace, and contains Turkish carpets, scattered pillows, tapestries of mythic scenes, candles in wine bottles, incense coiling up from brass urns, a globe, pipes, books, pens, ink bottles, drawings, clay bowls filled with pigments on an oak table, with a stool and painter's easel nearby. This appears to be an artist's studio from another era. He realizes he's been in this atelier before. Only he hadn't entered the way his guides had led him, but through a door behind a brocade curtain.

Pushing aside the curtain he steps into a room with a wall of stained glass facing him. Although the glass is virtually opaque because of its rich colors, he can make out citrus trees and an untended garden of tangled roses and morning glory amongst flowers gone wild. Looking around, he sees figures in the shadows, stretched out on low beds smoking opium. None of them looks over or says a word. A tall shimmering woman appears, lays an ice-cold hand on his neck, and points to a wooden box on the floor. Crammed inside the box, impossibly folded in, is another woman, staring up at him with a blissful gaze. The first woman begins sealing up this box with a hammer and green nails and indicates to the man she needs his assistance. Without question, he helps box up a number of pale yet ecstatic women, possibly to be shipped, or stored? The opium smokers seem to watch, but are in another world.

Soon he can take it no longer, leaps up, and returns to the other room. The tall woman chases him, grabs his shoulders and stares into his eyes. Her unlidded eyes have no pupils. She tells him she fears he is insane, and accuses him of stealing drugs from the Lab. Although he does feel a bit crazed, he knows he's not stolen any drugs and backs away, fully aware he's in the wrong place, feeling insubstantial, as if a character in a novel. Charging through the maze of labs, out of the valley and up onto a hill, he's startled to see the sun still rising. The same golden streaks covering landscape and farm, a faint pinkness in the eastern sky. Either time has stopped or it's at least one full day later. In any case, spotting the bright morning star rising above the horizon, he walks stealthily in its direction through the waving banners of time and space, knowing his destiny is in the "9."

SPACE IS THE PLACE

I MUST CRAWL OUT OF THE spacecraft, hand over hand on a lifeline connecting us with the asteroid we're mining. The rope is icy, slick, and so is the asteroid. I shakily collect an ore sample and return towards the ship. It is scary out here, hanging upside-down like a sloth over infinite blackness. I speak to the emptiness, "I do *not* want to do this again." I make it back into the capsule, feeling alone, isolated, despite the other crew members.

However, I *do* have to go out again, hopefully for the last time. As I'm half-way across, the cord breaks! and I float free, tumbling through space …

I'm with others in front of a giant wooden gate, perhaps 60-feet tall. The Gatekeeper is instructing us in *kung fu*. I'm not too good, and do many clumsy moves. The Master waves me over, shows me a sheet of my calligraphy, and with praise for my efforts says, "Perhaps you are not meant to be a fighter. Your writing is excellent. However, there are a few mistakes. It's *true*-maya not *faux*-maya." I blush at my ignorance, and apologize. He responds, "No need. I want you to inscribe these words on the gate. It's a reward for sincere hard work." I bow and thank him, go over to begin carving my text into the hard wood.

Back in the spacecraft after my narrow escape, I say in a serious voice to my fellow astronaut, "Igniting the salt recharges the battery." He stares at me quizzically, then stabs a syringe into my arm.

I'm climbing a wooden ladder attached to a stone wall, fearful the rungs will break, as the ladder must be thousands of years old. I'm retrieving a baseball-sized diamond from the top of the wall. I do this for a woman, waiting anxiously below. Afraid to look up or down, being many feet in the air, I finally reach the upper ledge, stretch towards the glittering jewel, and grab it! Carefully making my way down, the diamond secure in a pouch, I find the woman gone. I have no other choice but to climb back up again.

Revived by smelling salts, I peer up into the grinning face of the Gatekeeper, who says kindly, "It's OK to leave in mistakes. The *Tao* is like floating in space. No up, no down. But it is a *place*. Here where you are. Now." I sit up, croak thanks, weave over to the open gate, plunge through into *vast emptiness*.

IT NEVER ENTERED MY MIND

I'M OFF TO THE WINE STORE TO exchange a jug. But I become distracted, creating an abstract expressionist scene on a wall in shades of blue with splashes of red and black, entitled, "Ode to Bud Powell." Later, in the wine shop, I need change from the dwarf who runs the place. He snarls, "Change yourself." I respond, "All right, but I'll need a doorknob." The dwarf glares, his face all scrunched up, then goes back to fiddling with colorful mechanized insects on the counter that spin and fly dangerously around the room like angry bumblebees. At the back of the store, I finally discover a loose doorknob, grab it and shove it in my pocket before the dwarf looks up. With my prize secured, I hurry out, totally forgetting the wine exchange, and return towards home, where I intend to replace knobs.

At home I'm surprised to find a crow on the top step of the front porch. Instantly, as if awaiting my arrival, the bird begins a seemingly deliberate dance—taking two steps forward then two back, first leading with a left foot, then with a right, alternating back and forth. This appears to be a form of communication, but I don't get it. Bending over, I scratch the crow's head, stroke the blue-pearl sheen of its slick back, tickle its chest, ruffling feathers. Wanting to offer something, I dig into my shirt pocket and retrieve a fortune cookie, from dinner the night before. The crow acts insulted, screeches loudly and sails off over my head. Sitting on the porch, I break open the cookie, read the fortune: "Tough cookie, easy crumble." As I munch the cookie, a black feather slowly twirls to the ground.

Across the street, a tramp, huddled in a spacious overcoat, slouches on a park bench drinking from a brown bag. I saunter over and join him. He straightens, passes the pint of tokay and mumbles, "See that Caddy over there? That's *mine*." I regard the car parked nearby, a black El Dorado with gleaming chrome, and say, "Izzat so?" He explodes with laughter, choking and coughing, snatches the wine, and, with a sweeping gesture, one hand over his heart, proclaims, "I am the Prince of Denmark—*all* of this is mine!" He laughs madly again, so hard he falls off the bench. Reminded of what I must do, I shout, "Thanks!" catch a cab to the airport for the next flight out—to add a few more masterful touches to my change of scene, open that door into April, onto a stroll down a Parisian thoroughfare, just a little crazy.

BEINGS IN THE DREAM

A MAN IN A WHITE DRESS SHIRT and beige slacks sits on a sofa before a low coffee table in the living room of the family home. He stands and walks down the hall into the master bedroom. Then returns with a black-and-white photograph in his hand, sits back down on the sofa. After examining the photo for some time he slumps over on the couch and dies of a heart attack.

One of the man's children, a son, enters the room through the front door, finds a photograph on the carpet. Picking it up, he sees it is a picture of a man on his side on a couch, his feet on the floor, apparently passed out or sleeping in an awkward position. The man in the photograph is holding a photograph in his hand. The son of the dead man puts the picture in his pocket and, speaking loudly towards the other rooms of the house, says with varying, exaggerated intonations, "*I* am home. I *am* home. I am *home!*"

He goes into the kitchen and notices the dog has thrown up on the linoleum floor. Or at least that's what it looks like. He then pronounces, also in a booming "ritualistic" voice, "I am home ... *except* for this vomit." Hearing laughter he glances over at the breakfast nook. Allen Ginsberg is there, eating a bowl of granola.

Allen says, "Welcome to the threshold, pilgrim." The son goes over and joins the poet at the breakfast table. They both stare out the window at a gathering of hungry sparrows pecking in sparse winter grass patched with snow. A few crows stand nearby, cawing. The morning light is crystalline. Then the birds flutter away, and everything is utterly still—withered leaves on skeletal branches, gray horizon beyond. Just like a black-and-white photograph, thinks the son of the dead man.

A DIFFERENT TUNE

*A*FTER A LONG HOT DRIVE, I
stop to rest and get a drink at a saloon in a western "cowboy" town that
also has a gas station and general store, not much else. Entering, the first
thing I notice is everything's made of plywood—walls, floor, booths and
tables, even the bar itself, like it's all just been thrown together. A few
signs are prominently posted: *Rooms by the Nite, Drink Ducks Beer, No
Spittin.* Besides an old desert-rat in worn-out denims and battered
Stetson at the bar and the lady bartender, I'm the only one here. A dusty
amber light filters in through the open door, the windows shuttered up.
I order a *Ducks*, take a seat in a rectangle of light by the door, now aware
of old-timey music from an antique player piano on the other side of the
room, encased in shadows, cobwebs and dust.

Going over to check it out, I find it isn't a player piano, but something
out of a science fiction movie: Shaped like a hybrid of a samurai warrior
in black armor, a hurdy-gurdy, a 50s jukebox, and a sculpture by Max
Ernst, the machine gives off a distinct resonance of being alive, having a
"personality." It has rotating discs of primary colors imbedded in its
"chest," spinning and intertwining in such a fashion as to create the
music, or so I deduce. And the music isn't a ragtime piano score, but an
exceedingly complex composition with dramatic crescendos and inter-
ludes, like a Wagnerian opera of an epic creation story.

I'm overcome with a *déjà vu* sense of being transported to another
historical era. Maybe this magic jukebox only creates that impression, or
I've truly stepped into a "warp," I don't know—a terribly disturbing
sensation, nevertheless. I wobble over to the bar to question the bartender
and her other customer. As the old geezer seems in a drunken stupor, I

lightly tap him on the shoulder to get his attention. My hand goes right through him! He's made entirely of light. Looking aghast at the bartender, I realize she too is unreal, a projection from some hidden source. She merely stares at me blandly, waiting for my order.

Stunned, I return to the music machine to see if I can figure out how to play a different tune to somehow manipulate the scene, time and place. But the contraption is no longer there! Hearing its "rinky-tink" opera behind me, I whirl around to see the back of the hurdy-gurdy-samurai-sculpture striding through a "fuzzy space" in a wall. Running over, too late I encounter solid plywood, slapping my hand on it painfully hard to verify this fact. With a groan I wheel around, see my forgotten beer gleaming in the light. So I sit down, take a big swallow, methodically scan the now silent saloon, my heart beating wildly.

The "desert rat" swivels on his stool to face me, and begins speaking rapidly in a strange high voice—sounding like baby-talk, or someone attempting to speak a foreign language knowing only approximate rhythms, without any understanding of actual pronunciation or meaning of the words. The crusty old guy is excited, jabbering away as if telling me the most dreadfully important thing he knows. Yet, he isn't agitated or overly concerned, mainly wanting me to heed his diatribe, delivered in a frantically serious voice. He may be explaining what's happening here, what the "saloon" really is, but I don't get a word, and raise my shoulders and eyebrows with arms extended, palms up, in the universal gesture of "Don't understand."

My blank look and shrug of incomprehension don't deter the old-timer from his steady flow of intense chatter, delivered in such a childish, sing-song manner it makes me want to laugh; but I don't, too astonished to respond, and somewhat afraid, even knowing he's "only" light. Abruptly, he rises off the stool and glides towards me, still jabbering his nonsensical speech, comes over and sits down right into me! Startled, I look up from my beer—someone's changed the tune on the jukebox.

IN THE ZONE

"This can only be the end of the world, going forward." —RIMBAUD.

A SOLDIER IS BROWSING A flea market in the forbidden zone, when a young man with leprosy latches onto his leg with a vicious grip and won't let go. The soldier drags the poor leper over to a stall and buys a garish painting of idealized peasants on black velvet to bribe him off. All this to the cheering amusement of the leper's pals, also suffering from various malignant diseases, leprosy, elephantiasis, missing limbs blown off in the war, decay, insanity. He hands around all the *piasters* he has, and flees their clutching misery.

He's chasing around in burnt, ragged fatigues from one illicit market in the zone to another, looking for a special something. Finally he finds what he needs—for a few American greenbacks—an antique water-buffalo horn, intricately carved with scenes of the various levels of Heaven and Hell. The dealer, a crippled Frenchman with a bandaged eye, tells him it is blown to announce the Sacred Call to Battle. The man thinks, "Perfect. Mama-san will trade big time for this, number one, for sure."

Cutting through an alley to reach the *Bam Bam Club* before dark, he's ambushed by a gang of "cowboys" wearing Hong Kong suits and tennis shoes. They come at him with knives having hooked tips and cruel-looking serrated edges. He's so scared he doesn't notice an angel at his shoulder who removes him from that scene and deposits him in Hole Number One down behind the *Bam Bam*, where he finds himself squatting like a native in the stinking mud, bartering with black-toothed mama-san for a pound-bag of opium-laced killer weed.

Placing a black lacquered box on the ground before him, the old woman slides back the lid and removes a "Hail Mary" viper, deadliest in the world, then sets it down between his legs. He shows her a shit-eating grin, takes out the buffalo horn and gives it a toot. Instantly a dozen claymore mines are detonated along the berm, flares pop off around the perimeter, and he's behind his M-50 spewing streams of bloody fire into the hair-raising night.

"I won't go back there again, I swear it," the man says to a head impaled on a stake, just beyond the foot of his bed.

PASSION

*T*HROWN FROM A SPEEDING TRAIN, I land roughly in powdery dirt that billows up around me like a cloud. Standing, brushing myself off, looking around for someone or something familiar, I notice a sign above my head: *Ganges Depot*. To my open-mouthed astonishment, a bird-headed man with a long curved beak struts smartly out of the depot building and dips my hand into a bowl of red dye! I'm too flabbergasted to prevent this, nor when he takes my arm and pulls me over to press my handprint onto a stone wall covered with thousands of such red prints.

Recovering an ability to speak, I excitedly tell this new acquaintance all about the beautiful women of my home town—the blondes, redheads, the wonderful brunettes! boasting about my conquests, the mighty battles and fights I've won. Tagging after him, I'm babbling away, not paying attention to where we're going. Suddenly I lose him as we are swallowed up by an immense crowd of people gathered along a wide, sluggish, brown river. There's an endless number of funerals taking place along this river as far as I can behold. I am overwhelmed with nausea, stricken by the weeping and chanting in this swarming mass of grieving humanity.

Oily smoke from funeral pyres is so thick I cannot discern my hands nor my feet. A small clay bowl is abruptly thrust at me by a person swaddled in greasy rags. With a cautious sip, I'm relieved it contains a stimulating, thick green tea. Taking the brew, I sit down to rest beside a mound of smoldering bones to contemplate my situation. With a shudder that only renews my dizziness, I realize I must get home to my friends, my family, the beautiful women! "I must return *immediately*!" I yell, but I can't hear the words, which leave my mouth silently, even as my brain shouts them.

Rising on unsteady legs I weave a slow shuffle through dense packs of mourners and fire tenders. Like the bird-headed man, the latter appear not totally human, with either a head, or arms, hands or feet of various animals, fish, birds, snakes, as if God were playing random jokes with creation. Feeling tremendous pressure, hardly able to keep my head up, I drag my body back to the depot.

After this torturous effort, I crawl up to what appears to be the train station, but also seems a mirage, a painting on glass. Attempting to leap onto a train, I am flung upwards with great force, up into the flashing white sky. Then I am falling fast, screaming, grasping at the air, at clouds, at strange passing shapes, trying to hold onto something, *anything*, to catch myself, stop this horrible descent. But my thrashing struggles are in vain—as directly I see nothing—nothing but a bright light that "opens" me, and hear nothing—nothing but *Chatka! Chatka! Chatka!* all around and through me.

PROJECTIONIST

$\mathcal{A}$ GRAND OLD ART-DECO MOVIE house from the 20s is the only building still in use in a ruined part of town. Other buildings in the area are either boarded-up brick shells or demolished piles of masonry and rubble, inhabited by feral cats and dogs. Although the movie house is intact, it could collapse at any time—there are gaping cracks in the walls, and pipes and wiring can be seen where chunks of plaster have fallen out. The curtain, carpet, and seats are tattered, but no one minds, as the ambiance is warm, friendly and communal. I am caretaker of the theater as well as projectionist.

Before I roll the movie, people are invited from the audience to play a collection of unusual instruments as soundtrack. Some are actually ordinary kitchen gadgets like old egg beaters, mixers, waffle irons, that have been "adapted," others are natural objects I've gathered over the years, including shells, bones, and gourds. Many gladly come up to sit in the wings, banging or blowing on these "instruments," quickly learning how to make rudimentary music. Most get the hang of it, and synchronize into a Rube Goldbergian symphony of marvelous *bangs*, *bongs*, *rips*, *rattles*, and *roars*, sounding like a calliope from another planet.

Our movie tonight is an 18th-century silent film, thus the stirring background music doesn't interfere with any dialogue. After the film's in progress, I also go up on stage, where others from the audience have joined in a festive costume ball. I'm waltzing with a woman wearing an Empire gown revealing much pushed-up powdered cleavage. She has Popeye the Sailorman tattooed on one round breast and green spinach swirled in a pile on her head, draped over her shoulders, and tied above a white knee like a garter. I take the hint and remove my glass eye, revealing the "Eskimo mask of desire." I have a grizzly bear skin draped over my greased body, its head atop mine, which occasionally growls "sweet nothings" into her chartreuse beehive hair-do. Soon, the lady and I are amorously wrestling beneath the bear skin.

When the lights come on, after the movie ends with a burnt hole in the celluloid superimposed on the bleeding Marat, there are thousands of plastic yellow ducks floating around mid-air in the cavernous theater—and everyone exits with a jolly *quack! quack!* At the door I hand out flyers for next week's extravaganza, featuring clowns in exaggerated military uniforms, tongues and cheeks skewered like Indian fakirs, who engage in a turd fight with Art-World whores. Well, that's one idea. People express their pleasure or dislike for the experience they've just had by either kissing or punching me. Tonight was about half and half. Thus I'm "bruised by butterflies," as the poets say.

After the crowd departs, I climb onto the stage in my baggy, checkered "traveling" suit, and execute a slow, self-conscious, free-form cakewalk across the proscenium, lit only by a few footlights. Then, whirling in circles, I dance in ecstasy, leading into a loose-jointed boogie that carries me off the stage, up the aisle, and out into the empty street. Gazing up, I greet a fat yellow moon, tuck my head under my arm, and wend my way home. Happy to have been of use.

GENUINE HOODOO LADY

A FUTURISTIC HOTEL IN CAIRO has glass-and-steel pyramids juxtaposed with a rocket-launch station and a casino, but with overall elegance of the Taj Mahal. The clerks and bellboys look like medical technicians, scurrying around in white smocks, blinking boxes around necks, remote controls in gloved hands. My room's on the top floor—a magnificent suite, so grand I can't see from one end of the "space-age" living room to the other. The walls are gray-and-pink marble, floors black slate. An alcove attracts my attention with its monolithic darkness. Inside it I discover a recent excavation, as evidenced by the jumble of rock and debris on the floor.

Since no one else is around, I begin digging further into the hole someone's started in the alcove wall. This hole is perhaps two feet in circumference, dug into the solid rock at chest level. It's tough going, but I work hard and fast, chipping at the stone, then scraping dirt out beyond the rock. Feeling possessed of great energy and a determination to discover what's inside, I eventually force through into an open space.

Within this small hollow I find a perfectly smooth, white stone. Thinking it might be a dinosaur egg I split it open with a rock. But it's not an egg, it's a geode with flashing diamonds growing in its core. Despite the beauty and rarity of the stone, I sense this is not the sole treasure within. Returning to the pit I reach in deeper and pull out a bundle of papers and pamphlets wrapped inside a snake skin and tied with a gold cord. These writings must have been stashed here by previous explorers, as they have dates from the last to the present century, while the niche itself seems far older, perhaps from Dynastic times. The illustrated booklets describe various tonics, prayers, elixirs, and magic spells offered by a company called *Hours of the Tuat, Inc.*, in Memphis. One contains a grainy picture of an old woman wearing a flannel nightgown, whose face changes as I stare at it—from young to old, female to male, ugly to beautiful. The caption reads, "Genuine Hoodoo Lady Cures What Ails With Serpent Key."

Probing into the hollow again I grab a clump of curly black hair, long and soft, thus probably a woman's, and bound with a strip of folded cloth. The cloth has a pattern on it resembling hieroglyhics, but there isn't enough to be interpreted. I now believe the alcove was created before the hotel was built around it. My intuition tells me the papers were put here "out of time" and by the woman who set her length of hair inside as a sign and a seal, as her "signature." I am close to a break-through, to recovering what I've come here for.

Tying the length of hair around my throat I leave the alcove and step onto a balcony overlooking the city. The Sphinx and pyramids are just beyond, illuminated by a garish light show to impress tourists. I'm lost in a reverie, when suddenly an extension of the night, it seems, separates itself, comes forward, surrounds my body and holds me in an intimate, erotic embrace. There's no other way to describe it—I am enveloped by this feminine darkness, as if the essence of night itself is a woman, now gripping me tightly. I reel back into the room feeling this apparition become stronger, more aggressively seductive and sexual. Dropping onto the floor, I am making love to an enticing woman beneath me, enjoying her intoxicating desert perfume, her hot naked body clinging to mine, distinctly feeling myself enter her. When I do, this shocks us both, like we've hit more electricity than we can handle. Immediately, this female "darkness" slips away from me to reunite with the greater night outside, like a river pouring into the sea.

With a mingled sense of loss and exhilaration, I pack the "hoodoo" papers and geode in my satchel and leave the hotel. Soon I'm in a bustling bazaar, engulfed by the human noise of buying and selling, smoke, dust, odors of pungent spices, meat on braziers, dogs, camels, goats—a confluence of different tribal peoples. Wearing a coarse woolen robe, I'm playing a drum with a band of itinerant musicians and singers. I've passed through an important barrier and allow the rhythms of the drum to express my pleasure and satisfaction. Tomorrow we'll caravan to our village high up in the mountains. Our hearts break much too easily in the city—the killing pace, jarring sounds, polluted air and water, artificial lights—all sickness to the soul. We must return to Night's healing embrace.

THE STORIES OF OUR LIVES

*T*HE DESERT OASIS CONTAINS AN ancient yet living pomegranate tree that hasn't borne fruit for a century or more. Now gnarled and weathered, it provides little shade for my visionary enterprise: A small café and book store, where visitors may sit and relax, read a rare volume, or share the stories of their lives, while enjoying mint tea or an Arabian coffee with freshly baked pastries and bread.

Attached to the tree is a speaker from a tape player, which proclaims between selections of trance music from the region: Who's the dreamer? Who's the unborn? Who wants to know? Nobody offers the slightest response to these words. Or, if they do, their attention is directed only within themselves. The tree, I should mention, though seemingly barren, emits a riot of perfumes.

One unusually hot day, a vagabond, a limping stranger with a false leg, joins the regulars and other guests who've gathered for an afternoon meal and respite beneath the shade of my palm veranda. As a gift to everyone, by way of introduction, he hands around an exotic treat—pitted dates stuffed with hashish. As it turns out, each sweet also contains enough poison to kill a man. The assassin departs when everyone has slumped onto the tables or toppled to the ground, dead, except for me, spared because I recognized him and only pretended to eat his peace offering.

As he strides away, limping back out into the burning desert, I hear him sing in a high voice those "in-between" words played over the now-silent speaker in the pomegranate tree. His thin form shimmers like a mirage, a blue shadow rippling across the dunes, to vanish in a burst of light on the horizon.

Perhaps it is all a dream, and no one truly dies. Perhaps the vagabond is any one of us, heading towards the birth of the world. Perhaps the oasis exists overgrown somewhere in a great city, or there in the garden of the heart—ancient tree waiting to blossom once more. Perhaps time ended long ago, and there is only now, this present moment, where poetry, mystery, and uncertainty converge at an oasis café, where we converse over meals, share the stories of our lives.

BIOGRAPHY

*D*AVID DAHL, born in Los Angeles 1946, attended public schools, then UCLA 1964. Summer of 1965 hitch-hiked across country to New York City and back with fellow beatnik. Transferred to UC Santa Barbara 1965, home base, off and on, ever since. Married in January 1966, dropped out of school, went into Army, for reasons too obscure to explain. Mother dies of cancer February 1967. In Viet-nam March 1967 to March 1968, surviving the Tet Offensive. Remainder of Army duty in Germany near French border. In Paris during May 1968 riots. Divorced June 1969, same month as discharge. Return to university but unable to "adapt," considering recent past and on-going police riots and demonstrations on campus, including burning of Bank of America. Spent subsequent seven years either in brief forays in academia or on the road—two extended return trips to Europe, a summer in Mexico down to Yucatan, a year of Blakean studies in Reading, England, brief residence in Morocco. Eventually acquired BA in English from UCSB, 1976, and MA from San Francisco State University, 1978, where studied with Nanos Valaoritis and Stan Rice. Married artist Peggy Wirta in San Francisco, 1978, returned to Santa Barbara to work at various art and literary occupations. Father dies in August 1989. Won California Arts Council Fellowship in Poetry 1989. Poems published many places over the years: George Hitchcock's *Kayak*; *Minotaur* (SF); *Frank* (Paris); *Bouillabaisse* (New Hope); *Abraxas* (Madison); *Snakeskin* (Chicago); also *Sweet Little Sixteen*, a collection of American writers, published in Berlin; an anthology, *Life on the Line* (Mobile); and another, *Poetry and the Vietnam Experience* (St. Lawrence University); a chapbook, *Bright Garden At World's End*, 1996, Heaven Bone Press. A critical study of *The Other Room*, a collection of surrealist poems, appeared in a literary journal in Kyoto, Japan.